Our Special Christmas Joy

Sue Badeau

Helping Hands Press

ISBN: 978-1-62208-602-3

Foreword

Every year, a few days after Thanksgiving, a giant Christmas tree takes over our living room. For me the tree is always a chance to reflect on joy, memories from seasons past and my hopes for future generations of my family.

My husband, Hector, and I have been married for thirty-eight years. We've lived in seven cities in three states. We've crisscrossed the country many times, camping, with our children or for work. Every time we travel, we bring home a Christmas ornament as a souvenir. We have many now. Some handmade, rustic, shaped by children's hands challenged by cerebral palsy. Some, handed down from my great-grandmother Sue (who I am named after) are falling apart from age. Some are cheap, tacky, funny, silly, even goofy. Some are shiny and gaudy, while others are artistic, reverent, awesome and simple in their beauty. Each tells a story and holds a precious memory.

Over the years, here is how tree-decorating day would go at our house.

We'd start by making a big batch of homemade eggnog and my mom's shortbread cookies. Adult children arrive, teens emerge from their rooms. The smallest grandchildren prance and dance barely containing their excitement. Ornaments are laid out on our very large dining room table. Hector stands by the tree, with the ladder, ready to reach the high branches. I hover over the table, ready to hand out the ornaments. Adults and children line up, taking ornaments, one by one, and hang them on the tree. Christmas carols play in the background. We sing along. Sometimes we get rowdy. We laugh a lot. Sometimes we cry. We talk about the memories the different ornaments evoke.

Finally, the tree lights are turned on, all other lights extinguished and there is a hush. We sit down, quietly, and look at the tree. It holds so many memories - so many family members - birth parents, grandparents, three of our dear sons, a grandson and one great-granddaughter - who are no longer with us. So many places we have visited, people we have known, friends we have loved. Lessons learned, celebrations, challenges, griefs, sorrows, gladness and joy.

Front and center on the tree, a small ornament - not shiny, or fancy, simply made, quietly colored, beginning to fade - hangs from a bit of red ribbon. "JOY" it says, in cross-stitch. "Joy" is the theme of the tree, and indeed, of our family, in spite of all the hard times, the challenges, the sorrows - "JOY", indeed, stands front and center in our lives.

The little ornament on our tree is only displayed for a month or so each year. But the joy it represents is with us all year round. The joy that can be found in home-cooked pot of tortellini soup. The joy of watching children play soccer or hockey. The joy of scraping and painting a room. The joy of learning a new song on piano or violin. The joy of sitting by a cozy fire after a rousing snowball fight in the yard. The joy of listening to the newest baby gurgle and giggle.

Our "Joy" ornament is intact, and, although a little worn, has never been lost or broken, in spite of the many times our hearts have been a little lost or broken. Christmas is a time of joy, but sometimes in real life the moments of joy are interspersed with deep sadness, grief and an overwhelming feeling of loss. Our wish, our hope our prayer all is that all the joy God has given to us we may pass on to others bubbling up, doubled and tripled, overflowing like the waters that cover the sea. But before we can go there – we have to learn how to create joy amidst the broken pieces and in the broken spaces.

We learned this lesson well the year the tree fell over.

Imagine the horror and sinking feeling in the pit of my stomach when I came back to my hotel room after a speaking engagement a few years ago and called home to hear the news that the Christmas tree had toppled over, crashing down in our living room, shattering nearly all of the breakable ornaments. After recoiling in shock and disbelief, the tears started to flow. I was heartsick. My husband tried to re-assure me that he had salvaged many ornaments and it really wasn't as bad as it sounded. I held onto that hope as I continued my speaking engagements. It wasn't until I got home and surveyed the damage that I realized how many had truly been lost.

Thankfully, Hector had the foresight to sweep up and save the broken pieces. I stared silently into the box of brightly colored glass shards together with random limbs from ballerinas, reindeer and Shepherds and frantically tried to imagine a strategy to save these shattered symbols of so many memories. I invited my daughter SueAnn to come give me some tips. She is the most creative crafts-maker in the family and I had high hopes that she would say, "With my hot glue gun, I can fix them all – they will be restored and as good as new in no time!"

Alas, it was not to be so. She surveyed the mess and bluntly told me there was no way to put any of them back together exactly as they were before. "But," she brightly pointed out, "we could make mosaics and stained-glass type ornaments out of the broken pieces!"

What a terrific idea. We set to work and made several unique new ornaments to grace our tree. These new additions to our tree sparkle and catch the light in new and different ways than their predecessors did. They look different each time they are hung on the tree, depending upon the angle and proximity to the nearest light bulb. We have to dig a little deeper into our heart-memories to recall the specific stories, people and places associated with the bits of glass embedded in new settings. Mixing and matching has created some fun and unexpected quirkiness to our trips down memory lane.

While we were not able to make things "the way they were before," we were still able to make them "good as new." Beauty was created out of brokenness, and yet the brokenness was preserved with more integrity than sweeping it under the rug. We didn't try to create a fiction that the breakage never happened, but rather to acknowledge that we could still find beauty and the opportunity to restore JOY in the midst of the brokenness.

This, then, is the work of love. Not to pretend that grief, trauma or loss that creates havoc and sometimes shatters lives never happened. Not to sweep it under the rug and hope for a clean, fresh start. But to start with the broken pieces. Treasure them. Save them. Put them back together in new ways. Hold onto them old while re-fashioning them into something new. When we do this, there is hope. There is healing. Joy can be restored and made new.

Just as the Christmas tree goes up every year, so too do the stories and memories. Celebrating Christmas, Thanksgiving, Kwanzaa, and other holidays is one way to nurture and strengthen the roots of family ties. I enjoy writing stories with a holiday theme because the telling of stories allows us to see the times and places where we are most loved, where we exhibited strength, where God carried us across rocky terrain and where the seeds of hope for the future are planted and nurtured. Every tribe and community has its traditions for celebrating holidays and its own powerful storytelling tradition as well. From these tales come the wisdom and hope that nurtures and guides every people as they form the bridges that successfully link the past to the future through and over the sometimes muddy waters of the present.

I hope that as you read these stories you will be reminded of some of the moments of holiday joy in your own life– even joy that emerged out of messiness, disappointment or brokenness. Reflect on your own holiday traditions. Share the memories and stories with your children. Tell them stories of their ancestors and people. Gently guide them in telling their own stories.

As the popular song says, there are times when we all just "need a little Christmas" in our lives.

CONTENTS

1 HOCKEY SANTA

Chapter One

December 9

"Time to make the donuts." Homer Evers slowly hoisted himself into a sitting position at the end of the bed.

"I hear the words, but I don't see the sparkle—knees bothering you this morning?" Celia Evers stepped into the room in stocking feet, balancing a cup of coffee, her phone and a notebook.

"Knees? Yeah—head, shoulders, knees, and toes to be more accurate. This cold weather gets into my bones."

"Ahh, I see. And this coming from the man who used to get up at five in the morning, walk two miles while wearing skates and shovel the outdoor hockey rink for practice without complaining. You're getting old, Homer," Celia planted a kiss on his forehead. She set her things down and turned towards their shared closet to dig out a pair of shoes.

Emerging from the closet, Celia sat on the bed to slip on her shoes just as the phone vibrated on the nightstand. Dropping her left shoe, she pushed 'answer' and held the phone to her ear. Surprised to hear Commissioner Walter's voice on the other end, Celia pursed her lips waiting for the emergency of the day to be revealed. After listening for a few moments, she was relieved to learn that the crisis was a simple one to resolve. "No worries, Commissioner, Homer will be happy to do it. Check that off your worry-list for today. Oh, and just a reminder, I won't be in the office this morning, I have a home visit with the Cole family and then a meeting with the Inter-Agency Youth Transition Committee over in New Beckton."

Retrieving her shoe, Celia slid it on and stood up.

"Not so fast, missy. What did you tell your boss that 'Homer will be happy' to do?"

Celia laughed out loud when she saw the look on Homer's face. "Relax, it's nothing to worry about. Her husband was going to be Santa for the annual Christmas party we do for the kids in foster care, but now he has a conflict, so you get to do it. You were going to come to the party with me anyway, so I knew you wouldn't mind."

"I don't mind, it should be fun. I guess I'll have to add finding a Santa suit to my to-do list this week." Homer left the room to rouse the children for school, while Celia took her winter jacket off the hallway coat tree and stepped out into the cold.

~~~

Twelve hours later, Celia was finally home after a long day.

Hanging her jacket on the coat tree, her mind played back the challenging visit with the Cole family. Adoptive parents Ron and Evelynne were determined to stick with their plans to reunite their children, Jamie and Joanie, with their older sister Jennifer, but they described adding a teenager to their family like riding a wild bull at the rodeo. "Some days we feel like we are hanging on by a thread," Evelynne Cole had confided. Still, they truly grasped the importance of those sibling relationships and were not giving up. Celia could only hope that the resources she offered would ease some of the tensions in their home until things settled down.

She hated getting home so late, but she vowed not to let the stresses of the day impinge on family time. Tossing her scarf on the chair by the door, Celia stood stock still for a moment, inhaling deeply and relishing the welcoming aromas and warmth of the crackling fire, pot roast, and Christmas greenery. Peeking into the kitchen, she saw Rocky pouring juice and Dev feeding Sammy. CJ closed the refrigerator door, carrying ketchup to the table.

"Mom's home, Billy. Come on down to supper."

"This looks and smells wonderful, Homer." Potatoes and salad were passed around the table, forks clinked, CJ spilled his juice. Everyone laughed as Homer told a couple of funny stories from his work at Deanie's Diner.

Impatiently, CJ piped up, "Now can we tell her?"

Celia looked from face to face wondering what surprise CJ was waiting to reveal. Billy was oblivious to the conversation, digging into a second heaping plate of food. Neither Rocky's nor Dev's faces offered any hints but Sammy was smiling from ear to ear. Curious, Celia leaned forward.

"My sister called," Homer began.

"Aunt Lainey is coming for Christmas!" CJ added, "And she's going to bring those special candies!"

Celia turned this news over in her mind. On the one hand, it made sense. Homer's sister Elaine had taken their mother's death nine months earlier particularly hard, and just after Thanksgiving she fell, breaking her ankle. Unable to get out and about or participate in her church Christmas activities, she would likely be depressed spending the holidays alone in her small apartment. On the other hand, would the chaos of an Evers' Christmas be too much for her? It seemed she did best when enjoying this rambunctious family of eight in small doses. She liked peace, quiet, and order, all of which were in short supply any time of year at this house, but especially at Christmas.

As if reading her mind, Homer spoke up, "I called the Breckinridge. I remembered they had a guest house they sometimes make available for people to stay in temporarily. It's really quiet there, they have nurses on duty in case she needs anything and it's close to the Y so she can still swim every day— that's her favorite form of physical therapy for her ankle."

"Yeah, and Dad says I can drive her back and forth while she's here, so that'd be cool." Billy was apparently listening as he added his two cents to the conversation. Her newly-licensed son was always on the look-out for driving opportunities.

"So, it's settled. Now can I be excused?" Dev was already on his feet.

"Rocky, it's your night for cleanup. Scrape and stack everyone. And I expect to see homework before the TV goes on." Homer pushed back from the table and the kids sprang into action. Celia remained seated, content to watch the beehive of activity swirling around her for a few more minutes.

~~~

December 11

Homer pulled his car up into the circular front drive at the Breckinridge, gently easing to a stop. "Here we are," he said to his sister, scooting around the car to open her door and help her out. With her left leg still in a boot-cast, maneuvering was a bit of a challenge. Twinkling Christmas lights encircled the portico and a giant pine cone wreath dripping with miniature candy-canes adorned the front door.

Elaine Evers took it all in quietly, holding onto Homer's elbow as they slowly entered the well-lit receiving area. The first person to greet them was Opal Barnett. "Homer Evers, I heard your sister was going to join us for the holidays. I would know she was your sister from a mile away; the resemblance is striking."

"Hello Opal, great to see you. This is my sister, Elaine. You're right, people have always said our parents had mighty strong genes, we all look alike. It's that old Dutch stock, I guess." The three chatted briefly while waiting for an attendant to show Elaine to her room in the guest house on the west side of the back lawn.

Homer knew his sister was tired from a day of travel and eager to have a light supper before going to bed.

~~~

December 12

The next morning, Billy arrived at Breckinridge just after nine to drive his aunt over to see the family. They arrived just as Homer was pouring his second cup of coffee and Celia was clearing breakfast dishes. Taking her coat, Billy helpfully guided Elaine into the living room where CJ leapt up from the sofa and nearly tackled her with a boisterous bear-hug.

"Watch it, scamp," Billy cautioned. "She's got one broken ankle; she doesn't need you giving her another one."

Ignoring his brother's admonition, CJ couldn't contain his enthusiasm. "Guess what, Aunt Lainey?" CJ queried his aunt before she had a chance to sit down. "Dad is going to be Santa at the Christmas party for all the kids in foster care!"

Startled, Elaine stuttered, "Is that a fact?"

"We're all going, even you can come, too. We're going to have skating and hot chocolate with marshmallows and everyone gets a present."

"I wonder if your dad will wear a hockey uniform." Elaine said as she settled into a corner of the sofa.

"Aunt Lainey, I said it was a Christmas party, not Halloween, we're not wearing costumes. Well, dad is wearing a costume, because he is Santa, but it will be a Santa suit not a hockey uniform, silly."

Elaine turned to her brother and asked, "Homer, do you remember that one Christmas?"

Homer set his coffee mug on the edge of the bookcase and took off his glasses. Pulling his handkerchief from his back pocket, he mopped his brow, and then sat down across the room from Elaine and CJ. "I sure do, Lainey-Jean; how could I ever forget that Christmas?"

Chapter Two

Friday afternoon, Early December 1964

Sh-wop!

Homer jumped in his seat. The sharp crack of Sister Bernadette's ruler against his already raw knuckles stung, but he knew better than to cry. Boys don't cry. Pops said it nearly every day to Homer or one of his brothers. *"You want to cry, boy, I will give you a reason,"* Homer shuddered at the thought of his father's harsh words. He straightened up in his chair and looked up into the face of his teacher looming over him.

"Y-y-y-yes, sister?"

"Your paper, wah, ka-wah, blah-dey, waka waka blah . . . " Homer could not understand any of the sounds coming from Sister Bernadette's mouth, but she looked really mad. She stared at the blank worksheet in front of him, pointing with her ruler. Not wanting to be swatted again, he tried to smile, nodded, and picked up his pencil. He had no idea what she wanted him to do, but clearly she wanted to see him doing something.

The clock ticked slowly for the next two hours, but finally Homer was released from Sister Bernadette's clutches. He raced down the front steps of St. Martin's Elementary school, eyes wildly scanning the crowd for his big brother Roy. Spotting him across the street, Homer bolted, not waiting for an okay from the crossing guard.

Roy stepped into the street and yanked Homer to safety just

before a screeching car hurtled through the intersection. "Watch it Buzz; you want to be a hockey star, first thing you gotta do is stay alive." Roy used Homer's hockey nickname as he swatted his bottom with a rolled-up newspaper. "I ain't leavin' without you, you know Ma would kill me if I did. So slow down, save that speed for the rink."

Homer noticed three of Roy's friends, all members of the high school hockey team, chuckling a few yards away. His face suddenly felt hot and he knew it was turning bright red with embarrassment.

"We've got extra papers to deliver today. Pops signed me up for a second route so there would be more money for Christmas," Roy said, hoisting Homer onto the handlebars of his bike and slinging the newspaper bag across his chest. "But we still gotta git it done before hockey practice, so let's roll out."

Homer's eyes widened as he saw the overloaded newspaper bag. He hoped the extra money would be for Christmas but after hearing Ma and Pops fight last night, he was scared there wasn't going to be any Christmas at their house this year. And how were they ever going to do all these papers before hockey practice?

Roy peddled his bicycle with extra speed and the cold air stung Homer's chapped cheeks and hands. He wished he hadn't lost his mittens the last time he helped Coach Porter shovel the outdoor rink. Today, the brothers had a lot of ground to cover—the route always took longer on Fridays because they had to collect the money, and hopefully the tips, from their customers. Pops made

Roy turn over the paper route money to him for buying the family groceries, but they never told him about their tips. Roy squirreled away those extra dimes and quarters like they were pieces of gold. He especially liked old Mrs. Jenkins. Even though they had to carry the paper all the way up to her third floor apartment, she always left a whole dollar tip for Roy and a Baby Ruth candy bar for Homer. She was the last customer on their route.

"Do you think you could do this route by yerself, Buzz?" Roy asked as they climbed the steep staircase.

"All the papers, Roy? I—I—I don't know, I might be scared. Why are you asking me that?"

"Oh, I'm jist wondering. Yer gitting old enough now, I think. But don't worry, I don't mean next week or nothin', we'll stick together, you and me, for a while longer. Come'on now, we don't have much time and Coach Porter hates it when I git you to practice late."

~~~

Heading for the bedroom he shared with his three brothers after getting home from hockey practice, Homer didn't even want to go back downstairs for supper. He just wanted to curl up under the warm blankets and go to sleep. He nearly jumped through the ceiling when a hand reached out of the darkness in the hallway and wrapped around his wrist pulling him towards the girls' bedroom. Boys don't go in the girls' bedroom. Pops told the boys all the time, *"You got no business in there, boy. You need something to help you remember that?"*

"Shhhhhh, hush, come here Homer, I got something to show you." His sister Lainey quickly covered his mouth and closed her bedroom door behind them.

"But I can't be in here, Lainey," he whispered when she removed her hand.

"I know, that's why you gotta keep quiet." Lainey turned the light on and Homer blinked several times while his eyes adjusted. "Look what came today," Lainey continued, hoisting the thick Sears-Roebuck catalogue over her head, her eyes sparkling with excitement.

"Oooh, let me see it!" Homer jumped to snatch it from his sister's grasp but she held on tighter and giggled. After teasing him for a few more seconds, she sat down on the floor and opened the catalogue to the section with girls' dresses.

Homer plopped down beside her and whispered, "Come on, Lainey, turn to the toy section. You know you don't care about those girly dresses. You hate it when Pops makes you dress like a girl."

Lainey let Homer take control of the catalogue while she shimmied under the bed and emerged with an old composition book and a stubby pencil. "We gotta make the list, Homer. We gotta do it tonight so we have time to make our order." She wrote down the names of everyone in the family starting with Ma and Pops, then added their brothers Roy, Mitch and Howie and sisters Earlene and Debbie.

"Don't forget to put our names on there too, Lainey. Maybe

this year we'll have enough money so I can buy you somethin' and you can buy me somethin'."

"Prob'ly not, but I'll put our names at the bottom just in case. We can at least wish; that don't cost nothin'."

Homer continued paging through the catalogue and Lainey slid back under the bed. This time she crawled out with a thick sock in her hand. She turned it over on her lap, and several coins spilled out, along with two crumpled green bills. Homer's eyes widened when he saw that one of them was a five dollar bill.

"Where'd you git five dollars, Lainey? You didn't steal it from nobody, did you?"

"This is my secret babysitting money. I give most of it to Pops but I always keep a little saved for Christmas. Remember that time I stayed the whole weekend with those Orlow kids? That's when they paid me five dollars. And the dimes are from Earlene and Debbie when they pay me to make their bed. Have you been savin' your tip money? We gotta put our money together and see how much we got."

Homer thrust his hands into his pocket, pulling out two marbles, a stick of gum, half a Baby Ruth candy bar, three quarters, one dime and six nickels. The green marble rolled under the bed.

"That's all you got?"

"Roy keeps most of the tips, Lainey. You know I can't fight him about that. He'd whup me. But I'll have some more when our order comes in, I promise."

Lainey counted all the money and wrote down the total. For the next hour, the two sat hunched over the catalogue, picking out items for each family member. Lainey wrote every item number neatly on the page. They found gifts for their older sisters in the perfume section, a new apron for Ma, and GI Joe toys for Mitch and Howie. Finding something for Roy was harder, but they settled on a shiny comb and a tube of Brylecreem. Now that he was in high school and dating girls, he didn't like having to share the comb with his little brothers. They hadn't decided on anything for Pops when they heard footsteps in the hallway.

"Quick Homer, git under the bed."

Homer slithered under the bed in the nick of time before Pops opened the door. The smell of Canadian Club preceded him into the room. The dust under the bed almost made Homer sneeze, but he clasped both hands tightly over his nose and mouth, desperately trying not to make a sound.

"Git downstairs and help yer mother with supper, Lainey. And find Homer. I ain't seen that little rascal since he got back from hockey. He's going to see the backside of my belt if he don't git his hockey bag down to the basement before supper."

Lainey waited for several seconds after Pops' footsteps receded down the stairs before giving Homer the 'all clear" signal to come out. "We'll finish our list in the morning and then I'll go make the order while you help Pops with the groceries," Lainey said, tucking the catalogue and notebook out of sight.

"Our list is finished, Lainey-Jean. Pops is drinkin' again so I don't want to git him nothing," Homer said as he scampered out of the room.

"Father Jeremy wouldn't like that attitude, Homer Evers," Lainey called after him as she walked toward the stairs.

Chapter Three

Saturday, Early December 1964

Homer tiptoed into the kitchen, his bare feet freezing against the cold linoleum floor. After smelling the whiskey on Pops' breath last night, he didn't know what to expect this morning, but he sure didn't want to be the one to wake him up if he was still sleeping. His brothers Mitch and Howie were already at the table gobbling up their steaming bowls of oatmeal flecked with raisins. Ma was kneeling on the floor, her arms elbow deep in a bucket of soapy water. No sign of Pops.

"Who will be buying groceries today?" Homer wondered aloud. When Pops wasn't drinking, he always took Homer on Saturday mornings to buy the family's food for the week. If he was in a good mood, he would stop by Jimbo's Diner for coffee and Homer always got a donut. But when Pops was on a bender, the older girls usually did the shopping and it was never any fun to go with them.

"You are, boy. You and me, like always," Pops' booming voice called out from the living room. "Don't eat no oatmeal, I expect we'll stop at Jimbo's before we come home." Homer scrambled away from the table and hurried to get dressed before Pops changed his mind. Saturday morning shopping was his favorite and he didn't want to mess it up. As he charged down the stairs to get his snow boots and winter coat out of the basement, he heard Lainey telling Ma she had to babysit for the Orlow kids today.

Homer knew that wasn't true. Lainey planned to take their list and go to the Sears-Roebuck store to put in their order. She had to do it today to make sure everything would come back in time for Christmas. Homer suddenly felt bad about telling Lainey not to get a gift for Pops, but he knew she would get him something anyway. Lainey was like that. Too soft sometimes even when she tried to be tough, 'rastling and playing hockey with the boys.

He also knew she hated lying to Ma about babysitting, but he wouldn't tell. Homer was good at keeping secrets. If they didn't order the gifts today, there likely would be no gifts under the tree. Ma always made everyone a new set of mittens and hat and wrapped 'em up just so they would have somethin' to open, but it was never the same as the way the kids at school talked about. Santa brought them bicycles and new skates, dolls, and real Tonka trucks every year. Santa brought their mamas beautiful necklaces and fancy shoes, and hunting gear for the fathers. But Santa skipped the Evers' house some years. That's just how it was. Even Father Jeremy didn't really have no good explanation for it. Homer hoped he could talk to Santa directly one day and find out.

"You ready, boy? I'll leave without you if you ain't in the car by the time I count to five!"

Homer made it to the car before Pops got to four. It was going to be a good day. Pops turned the key and the engine sputtered and growled. It always took extra time to start up in the winter. Pops waited a few seconds and tried again. This time it took and cold air streamed out of the blowers onto the window. Pops handed Homer a plastic scraper and told him to scrape the ice off the back window while he did the front. A few minutes later, his hands nearly numb, Homer slid back into the front seat ready to go. He eyed the glove compartment and then looked up at his father.

Pops laughed. "Go ahead boy, have a mint. Git one fer me, too." Homer popped the sweet sucker into his mouth as the car swung out of the driveway and headed south of town for the discount food market. They always went on Saturdays because the day-old bread was on sale for a dime a loaf. Some weeks they came home with more than twenty loaves of bread. It wasn't as good as the bread Ma made with raisins, but the extra loaves sometimes meant French toast for Sunday morning breakfast.

It took more than an hour but finally they finished loading the grocery bags into the car. Homer waited anxiously to see if Pops still planned to go to Jimbo's Diner. Pops must have been thinkin' about it hard because he sat there in the parking lot for a long time before turning the key so they could leave. Finally, he turned to Homer, "Ready for a Jimbo's donut, son? Let's git on over there."

Homer's excitement was short-lived. They sat down at the counter and Miss Maybelline poured coffee for Pops. But then Walter Furness walked in and sat right down next to Pops. He smelled something fierce and looked worse. "Heard they laid you off down the plant, Evers; is that the truth?"

Pops looked like he wanted to kill old man Furness, but he just nodded. "Don't talk about that in front of my boy, Walt, or we'll be steppin' outside."

"Aw, lay off man, look, I brought you some sweetener for yer coffee." Furness flashed his toothless grin and pulled a flask out of his coat pocket. Pops took it and poured a hefty swig into his coffee. He slapped the old man on the back.

"I guess you ain't so bad, Furness. I'll let you live another day." On that note, everyone in the diner started to laugh, except for Homer. He hunched down over his donut and his lip quivered. But he wouldn't cry. No sir. Boys don't never cry.

Chapter Four

Wednesday, Two weeks later

Both Roy and Lainey were on the corner already when Homer burst through the doors of St. Martin's School ready to tackle the paper route and get to hockey practice. Mitch and Howie trailed behind him. Homer guessed that they were hoping to sneak in some time on the school playground before Lainey walked them home to start on their chores. He did a double-take when he saw that Roy was straddling his own bike and holding onto another one.

Before Homer could ask Roy about the second bike, Lainey grabbed his arm and pulled him to the side. "Give me the rest of your money. I'm walking over to Sears-Roebuck again today to see if our order is in," she whispered.

"It wasn't there on Monday. Did the postcard come in the mail yet?" Homer asked.

"Shhhh, don't let Roy hear you. No. The postcard didn't come, but I'm going to check anyway so give me all the money you have from last Friday's tips. Be smart. Don't let Roy see you. It's our secret." Homer dug the few coins he had out of his pocket and handed them to his sister. His fingers were stiff and cold. Lainey stuffed the money in her pocket and crossed the street in search of Mitch and Howie.

"Hurry up Buzz, what's takin' so long? I have a surprise for you today," Roy called out. Homer trotted over to where Roy stood with the two bikes. The second bike was red and a little rusty. The plastic sleeve was missing from one of the handlebars and the reflector light on the back was cracked.

"Whose bike, Roy?"

"Belongs to my friend, Joe Aikens. His kid brother broke his leg out hunting last week, so he can't use it for a while. So you can use it for a couple weeks. Don't get attached er nothin'; you can't keep it. But now that I got you a bike, you can do the paper route yerself."

Homer lunged for the bike, testing the horn and patting the cracked vinyl seat. He'd never had a bike to ride before. He always had to sit on Roy's handlebars. He knew how to ride, a'course. Roy taught him last summer, but riding around the town streets? By himself? Homer shivered.

"I don't know if I can do that route myself, Roy. I'm scared. What if I mess up? Or what if I get lost? Or what if I…?"

"Slow down, little brother. You know the route. I bet you could do it blindfolded. And you didn't git that nickname Buzz for nothin'. Yer the fastest kid on the hockey team, I know you got speed. You have to do it. But it's our little secret, OK? Don't tell Ma, she'll kill me. And don't be telling Pops neither."

"But I don't understand, Roy. What are you going to do if I gotta do the route myself?"

"You ask too many questions, kid. I got stuff to take care of. Now that Pops isn't working, I gotta be the man of the house. Jist do what I tell you. Deliver the papers. Go to hockey practice like always. Then when yer comin' home, stash the bike out back by the shed before you come inside. Make sure Ma and Pops don't see you. You can keep a secret, can't you Buzz?"

"I—I—I guess so, Roy. I'm gonna try my best."

"That's the spirit." Roy slung the paper bag over Homer's thin shoulders. That's when Homer noticed Roy had another bulging newspaper bag hanging from his own bike.

"Do I do the first route, Roy, or both the routes we been doing the last two weeks?"

"Both routes, and don't forgit, Pops is counting on that money, so don't miss any houses." With that Roy hopped on his bike and rode away toward the east side of town.

East side? That's where the rich kids live, what's Roy going that way for? Homer wondered. He climbed onto the red bike and wobbled away. Balancing the newspaper bag and remembering how to ride wasn't so easy. He almost veered into the road before swerving back and hitting the curb so abruptly he fell off the bike, landing hard on his shoulder. Newspapers tumbled out of the bag. The wind was picking up so he had to collect all the papers before they blew away. Homer's nose started to run. Now he was really going to be late for hockey practice. *Why is Roy doing this to me?*

Homer knew the answer to his own question. *He knows I can keep a secret, that's why.* Homer got back on the bike and tried again. This time, he managed to keep everything right-side up and soon he was turning onto Maple Avenue where the paper route started. One by one he delivered the papers until finally arriving at

Mrs. Jenkins' place. He dropped the bike into the snow and headed up to the third floor. By the time he got back outside it was nearly dark out. If he rode really fast, maybe he could still make it to practice on time. He didn't want to disappoint Coach Porter by being late.

His fingers and ears were burning from the cold, and his toes where numb when he got to the rink and plopped down on the wooden bench to lace up his skates. His teammates were already on the ice. It was so hard to lace his own skates. He never got them as tight as when Roy did it for him. He liked them nice and tight so he could skate hard and fast and not worry about wobbling and ankle-skating like Terrence Newcomb always did. Finally, he was ready to take the ice.

All fear, anger, and worry left Homer the minute he glided onto the ice. It was like he stepped out of his real life and into another place, a place where he was brave and strong and nothing could stop him. He flew around the rink, lap after lap, warming up and proving once again that he deserved his nickname. *No one can catch me!* Homer couldn't wait until it was his turn to skate for the high school team like Roy. He even hoped he'd be able to wear the same number nine jersey that Roy wears. With the hockey stick in his hand, he forgot how cold and chapped his fingers were as he swatted at the puck again and again. Thunk! Thunk! Thunk! Puck after puck hitting the backboards with such satisfying speed and power.

Maybe Pops will stop drinking by the time I am on the high school team. Maybe he'll come and watch me and say, "That's my boy."

Homer didn't want practice to end, but soon it was too dark and too cold for the boys to stay on the ice any longer. Coach Porter gave them a final reminder about Saturday's game while they unlaced their skates. Homer stared across the parking lot as the mothers and fathers of his teammates drove in to pick up their sons. He wished he was climbing into a warm car. But at least he had a bike today. That was better than walking home. Terrence Newcomb had to walk. He lived even further down the river than the Evers' family. He didn't even have a father. *Maybe it would be better to have no father than a father like mine.*

Homer gasped at his own thoughts. He knew he would have to tell Father Jeremy about this in confession. *I'm sorry Father, I have sinned. I thought horrible thoughts about my Pops. I am a bad son.* He hopped on the red bike and began peddling wildly towards home.

Homer stashed the bike behind the shed and walked around the bushes toward the front door. At the same moment, Lainey was walking back towards the shed, laden with packages. "The order! It came!" Homer blurted out with delight.

"Shhhh. Hush. You want everyone to know our secret? Help me hide these packages in the back of the shed," Lainey instructed.

Homer froze. If Lainey went back there she would see the bike. What would he say? He had promised Roy he could keep a secret. He had an idea. "Lainey, you know Ma needs you to help with supper. You go on inside before Pops comes out here looking for you. I'll hide the packages. You can count on me."

"Well for once you have a good idea, Homer Evers. I think that's exactly what I'll do." Lainey dropped the packages at Homer's feet and turned to walk towards the front of the house. Phew! Homer was relieved. All the secrets were safe for one more day. *I hope I can keep the secrets safe all the way until Christmas.*

Chapter Five

December 24, 1964

"Ouch!" Homer woke up to the crunch of an elbow whacking his ribs. Mitch and Howie were jumping and horsing around on the bed.

"Wake up, Homer! Wake up! It's Christmas Eve!" the younger boys shouted nearly in unison.

"Shhh. Don't wake up Pops or it won't be very merry," Homer replied. He glanced around the room. Roy was already gone. "Where did Roy go?"

"He don't tell us nothin'," Mitch said.

"He just up and left before it was even light out," Howie added.

"No school today. Let's go get breakfast and then maybe we can go out and skate."

The three brothers scampered down the stairs. The kitchen smelled like cinnamon. Ma stood at the stove making French Toast. A fresh batch of her cinnamon sugar cookies sat cooling on wire racks on the counter. Homer couldn't help himself. He reached out his hand and snatched one of the plump, soft treats, popping it in his mouth quickly before anyone could stop him.

"You rascal, Homer Evers. Those cookies are for tonight before Mass," Ma scolded, swatting his hand with the spatula, while Mitch and Howie each grabbed a cookie of their own. "Now, see what you started."

"I'm sorry, Ma." Homer said the words but the warm sweet

taste of sugar cookie lingered in his mouth and he wasn't sorry at all. He couldn't believe she made cookies and French Toast on the same day. Maybe this Christmas would be a little merry after all. Maybe Santa wouldn't skip their house this year.

Lainey walked into the kitchen still in her pajamas. "You boys better shush. Earlene and Debbie don't want to get up yet. They said it's the only day they can get their beauty sleep. They told me to tell you Santa won't come if you keep this racket up."

"Oh they ain't got nothin' to do with Santa. They just like to be bossy," Mitch said, and Howie laughed, spewing cookie crumbs at Lainey.

"Yuck, Howie. You have no couth."

"What's couth?"

"See, you don't even know what it is."

"Ma, what's couth?"

"Oh, you never mind about that. Get your plate and eat some French Toast. Then Homer can take you boys over to the rink to skate a while, burn off some energy. It's a long wait until midnight Mass. Oh and don't forget to bring down a sock so we can hang it on the railing for Santa." Ma slid a plate of French Toast in front of each boy and Lainey followed adding a small sprinkling of powdered sugar. There was no money for syrup this year.

~~~

Nearly four hours later, the boys returned, tromping through the kitchen, melting snow dripping on the floor in their wake. "Get those wet smelly clothes down in the basement," Debbie said. She was perched on a stool at the kitchen table smoking a cigarette and looking at a magazine. Earlene stood over her, rolling Debbie's hair up in curlers.

"Oh good Homer, you're back, come give me a hand here." Ma had the step ladder propped against the stair railing, with a hammer in her hand and a bunch of old socks slung over her shoulder. One by one, Homer and Ma tacked the socks to the railing.

"All ready for Santa," Homer said hopefully.

"Don't forget, Homer. Even when Santa passes us by, Jesus never does. He comes every Christmas and blesses us for another year."

Homer understood the meaning. Santa would be 'passing us by' again this year. He bit his lip and willed himself not to cry. He and Lainey had snuck out of bed late last night while everyone was sleeping to wrap the gifts from Sears-Roebuck. They didn't have enough money left this year to buy gifts for each other but he still couldn't wait to see the looks on his brothers and sisters faces when they discovered there were presents for them even without Santa. *Who needs Santa anyway?*

Homer walked into the living room. Pops snored on the sofa with his mouth open. The TV was turned on to a hockey game. Homer had just figured out who was playing when Earlene and Debbie walked in, both heads piled high with fat curlers. Debbie walked over and changed the channel. *Miracle on 34th Street* was on.

"Yer gonna get whupped if Pops notices you changed his

hockey game," Homer said.

"Does it look like he's going to notice? Just keep quiet and we can have a little Christmas fun dreaming of going out on dates with Fred Gailey," Earlene joked.

"I'd like to be Susan," Lainey added, offering her own Natalie Wood imitation. *"I believe, I believe. It's silly but I believe."*

"I'd like my hair to look like Maureen O'Hara's. Do you think you can comb it out like that after it sets?" Debbie asked.

"I wish the real Kris Kringle would come here. But we always get the drunk Santa," Homer said.

"Watch your mouth, boy. Yer gonna wake him up." All six youngsters stopped talking and gazed at the television, each lost in their own fantasy.

Darkness descended on the town and the little house on Bolton Street, only the glow from the television providing light. Lainey plugged in the lights on their Christmas tree just as Fred recited Homer's favorite line in the movie, '*Faith is believing, even when common sense tells you not to.*' The aroma of Ma's famous Christmas Eve stew filled the house. Everything looked softer and more magical with the Christmas lights on. Even the old socks on the stairs looked less dingy.

The movie ended and Ma stepped into the room. She was still wearing her old stained apron. Homer couldn't wait for her to open the new one tonight. She would be so happy and surprised. "Scoot. Git to bed. You only have a few hours to sleep before midnight Mass. I don't want none of you snoozing in church. so go take yer naps now." Ma switched the TV off and shooed her children up the stairs. Even the teenagers had to go to bed on Christmas Eve.

Homer fidgeted in bed. He didn't think he would sleep. He was too excited about giving out the Sears-Roebuck gifts. He imagined Earlene and Debbie trying out their new perfumes. He smiled thinking about Mitch and Howie playing GI Joe. And Roy would be so surprised with his Brylecreem. His eyes fluttered closed. *Where is Roy?* He wondered just before drifting off to sleep.

Chapter Six

Christmas Eve, 1964

Mitch and Howie giggled in the hallway. Lainey and Homer quietly stood near the top of the stairs awaiting the word from Ma that it was time to come down for Christmas Eve supper and to get ready for Mass. Earlene and Debbie had gone down ahead to help Ma. Roy was still not home.

"Come down!"

The whole house hummed with excitement. The socks on the stairway bulged with goodies. Lainey and Homer quickly slipped into the hall closet to retrieve the bag of wrapped gifts they had hidden earlier in the day and placed them under the tree. In the kitchen, the table was set with the good plates and Earlene poured homemade egg nog into fancy tea cups. The family gathered around the table. Pops sat in his usual spot, not talking or smiling, but not drinking yet either so Homer let out the breath he'd been holding deep in his belly.

"Let's pray," Ma said.

"Are we going to eat supper without Roy?" Homer asked in disbelief. Surely they couldn't start Christmas without Roy.

"Father Jeremy needed him early at church," Ma said, adding, "We'll see him when we get there."

"Is Father Jeremy saying Mass on Christmas Eve? Isn't it usually Monsignor at Midnight Mass?" Lainey asked. All of the Evers' kids loved Father Jeremy the best. He made Catechism fun and he sometimes added surprising things to Mass, like different music, and once he played his guitar. During Mass!

"Monsignor is saying Mass tonight, Lainey, but Father Jeremy is helping and he said he has a surprise to make the Mass more interesting for children. So he wanted Roy to help. Now, let's pray so we can eat."

Mitch and Howie finished their stew before Ma even had a chance to sit down. "Can we open the stockings now, Ma? Please?" Both boys had already jumped out of their seats and moved towards the stairs.

"Git back down over here and let your mother eat, boys. Those socks ain't going anywhere. Sit."

"Yes, Pops," Mitch said and the two brothers rejoined the family at the table.

Homer noticed Ma had served herself a very small portion and she finished eating in no time. Soon, everyone scrambled for their socks, pulling them off the railing and darting into the living room to reveal the treats inside. Each stocking held a brand new winter hat, scarf and pair of mittens—a different color for each child. Two candy canes, a handful of walnuts and a few of Pops' special mint suckers completed the package. No toys for the boys. No fancy hair combs or jewelry for the girls. Still, no one complained.

"Look! There are presents under the tree," Mitch exclaimed. Trotting over to take a closer look, he said, "Our names are on these packages. Can we open them?"

Homer stole a glance at Ma and Pops. They were honest-to-goodness surprised. This was what he had been waiting for. He nearly burst out of his skin. Mitch and Howie passed the presents around. No one seemed to notice that Homer and Lainey didn't have one, they were all so entranced with their own gifts. It was exactly the way he imagined. Mitch and Howie were playing GI Joe, Earlene and Debbie were trying out their perfume and Ma was modelling her new apron with tears in her eyes. Even Pops seemed to like the new socks Lainey had picked out for him. If only Roy was here it would be perfect.

Just then the front door flew open and a gust of cold air filled the house. "Ho! Ho! Ho!" A deep voice called out and suddenly Santa was in the middle of the living room, passing gifts out to everyone, including Lainey and Homer. Homer couldn't believe his eyes.

Lainey repeated the line from the movie, "*I believe. I believe. It's silly but I believe.*"

Homer stared and stared at Santa. He had on a red hat and a red jacket and a very white beard. But his pants. His pants sure looked like hockey pants. Not just any hockey pants. Roy's hockey pants. *Could it be? But Ma said Roy is at church. I don't know what to think. Could Santa really wear hockey pants?*

~~~

Thirty minutes later, the Evers family arrived at St. Martin's Church for Midnight Mass. Roy was waiting for them by the front door, his cheeks blazing red.

"Roy! You'll never believe what happened! Where have you

been all day? You missed everything."

Roy mussed up Homer's hair, whispering, "You'll have to tell me about it after Mass. Let's git inside, it's mighty cold out here."

When it was time for the Liturgy of the Word, Father Jeremy stood. "I promised the children a surprise tonight," he said. He went to the side door and opened it. In came people dressed up in costumes. Mary and Joseph. Shepherds, Wise Men. And real live animals. They stood silently in front of the church while Father read the gospel story. And then he got out his guitar.

"We're going to sing a different song tonight. It's called *The Friendly Beasts* and you all have a copy, so I hope you will sing with me. Before I start, I want you to look at the first line. *Jesus our brother, kind and good.* If you have a brother, if you have a sister, I hope you will take a moment on this beautiful Christmas Eve to tell them you love them. Jesus is our brother, kind and good, but he also gave us brothers and sisters here, to walk on this earth with us. Your brothers and your sisters love you deeper than friends and they are always with you, in good times and in bad. Hug your brothers and sisters tonight. Hold on tight. Never let go."

Homer reached for Roy's hand on his left and Lainey's hand on his right. *I'm never letting go. This is the best Christmas ever.*

Epilogue

December 12

"Wow, what a cool story. Now I see why you asked if Dad was going to wear a hockey uniform to the Christmas party, Aunt Lainey!" CJ bounced up and down on the sofa.

"What did I miss?" Celia walked into the living room just as the story ended.

"It's a secret, mom, and dad sure is good at keeping secrets." Homer and Elaine laughed along with CJ, while Celia looked from one face to the other completely perplexed.

"I was just thinking about two things," Homer said, standing up and stretching out his stiff leg, "First, I want to thank you, Celia, for how hard you work to help the siblings in foster care stay together, or to reunite them when they are separated. Even when it is tough, I know you go the extra mile for those kids and I just want you to know—it matters. Lainey has reminded me of how powerful and important those relationships are."

"Hear, hear!" Lainey chimed in, "When you have good brothers and sisters, you never want to let go."

"And the second thing?" Celia asked.

"Do you know where my old hockey uniform is? I think I'm going to be needing it for that Christmas party next week."

2 THE CHRISTMAS PRIMER

Chapter 1

August 29, 1864

Titus gave Maudie's teat one last pull and stood up, hoisting the pail of warm milk with both hands. The dry straw crunched under his feet as he walked past Maudie's newest calf and headed for the barn door. His older cousin, Ellie Peters, poked her head inside the barn, surprising Titus and nearly causing the milk to slosh out of the pail.

"Why Titus King, that there is not near enough milk for your momma. She could barely squeeze a pound of butter out of that. You best git yerself back over to Miss Maudie and fill yer pail up to the top. You know yer momma will send you right back out here if she sees that. They got to churn enough butter to bring down to Dunham's before nightfall."

Titus didn't know why he'd been so excited when momma told him that Ellie was coming up from the bottom of the hill to spend the day. All she ever did was boss him around, especially now that her daddy, Uncle

William, got himself sent off to war. Titus looked at the door of the house, licking his lips and almost tasting one of his momma's biscuits with jam, his usual reward for helping with the barn chores. He set one foot down outside the barn door, ready to head to the house, but took another look at Ellie with her arms wrapped across her chest and remembered Momma telling him he had to be nice to her, seeing how she was sad about her daddy being gone. And he knew, too, that Momma would be mad if he showed up with just half a pail of milk. He turned around and trudged back towards the milk cow.

"I'm sorry Maudie," Titus said, sitting again on the upside down pail he used for a seat in the barn, "I was trying to help you save some milk for that new baby of yours, but I guess my momma needs it for butter. That's such a pretty new baby. Poppa says I can give her a name. What do you think we should call her?" Maudie turned her head and looked at Titus, letting out a deep, low mooing sound as if in response to his question. "Maisie you say? I was thinkin' the same thing." Titus said, gently slapping the big momma cow on her hindquarters. "I'll tell Poppa and Momma the new baby has a name."

This time when Titus stood up, the milk pail was so full he could hardly lift it. It was a struggle to carry it more than half a dozen steps before he had to set it down and rest. The distance to the house sure did look a lot longer all of a sudden, and the heat from the late August sun raised sweat beads on his back and forehead. It was so hot even the flies were too lazy to trouble him. He heard their low hum back by the animals, but he didn't have to shoo many away. Ellie must have run along ahead of him. He didn't see her anywhere in the yard.

Titus set the pail down for the third time about halfway to the house. His shoulders were starting to burn. Ellie shot out of the house and ran to him. "I'll help you with that pail, Titus," she said, catching her breath. "We need to git inside the house quick; yer momma has a visitor." She slipped her hand next to his on the wiry handle of the pail, and they walked quickly in step to the house, only spilling a little milk along the way. Three barn cats trailed after them happily lapping up the milk droplets on the leaves of grass and clover. The sky was an unbroken span of bright blue, with not a single white cloud to provide a moment of shade.

The King family had visitors nearly every day, so Titus couldn't understand why Ellie was fluttering so. So many of the men from the hill community were off at war, it wasn't unusual for the womenfolk to gather at one house and help each other with the churning, sewing, gardening, and other chores. But something seemed different about Ellie's manner, and so Titus wondered who the mystery guest could be. He hoped it wasn't someone coming to get his poppa for the war. Poppa had that gimp leg, plus he was forty-six years old now, and he told Titus they were only taking men up to the age of forty-five. But still, seemed like every week a few more men were leaving the hill, and so far none had come back.

Titus's stomach twisted inside as he took the heavy milk pail over next to the icebox and looked around. Only Ellie's momma, Aunt Charlotte, had come to help with the chores. She sat at the spinning wheel next to a pile of shearings from the sheep. Momma stood by the table next to a pale woman, pouring some lemonade.

"Who is the visitor?" he whispered through his teeth to Ellie.

"That's Miss Miller. She's our teacher at the schoolhouse. She's all grown up, but she's not married, and she doesn't have any children. She says the pupils at the school are her children."

Titus opened his eyes wide while Ellie spoke. Did this woman snatch other people's children? He didn't want to go with her. Maybe she was mad because Ellie escaped. Titus knew that it was not safe for people with dark skin to escape. Poppa had told him that story so many times. "Is she mad at you, Ellie?"

"Naw, she likes me. I was one of her best pupils last year. I learned my whole primer faster than the other children. I like school. My momma says it's about to be time for school again. She says we can go some days, but with the men all gone to war she ain't sure if we can go every day this year."

"You don't have to stay with Miss Miller?"

"Course not, silly. Why would you say that?"

"You said she wants her pupils to be her children."

"Oh, Titus, not her real children. She just looks out fer us during the day when we're at the schoolhouse. Then we all go to our own houses."

"Titus, put that milk down and come over here please." Titus looked up to see his Momma holding her hand out towards him and waving him over to the table. He didn't realize he still clutched the milk pail tightly with both hands. He set it down and scampered quickly over to her side.

"This is my boy Titus. Stand up straight and tall, Titus," Momma said. Titus stretched his back and lifted his head. Miss Miller looked up and down from his nose to his toes.

"Hello Titus. I'm Miss Miller. I've come today to make sure you'll be joining us when school starts in September. That's just two weeks away. Would you like that?"

Titus looked at his momma. He didn't know if he should say yes or no. He held his breath for a moment, not knowing what to do.

"Titus will make a great pupil, Miss Miller. I heard his cousin Ellie was a star student last year, and I expect nothing less from my son Titus."

Titus let his breath out in a whoosh. He heard Ellie giggle from the other side of the room.

"That's wonderful, Titus. Mrs. King, you and Mr. King have no other children?"

Momma's face looked tight. Her eyes fixed on a spot by the cook stove. Titus shivered. It looked like Momma had left out of herself and gone to that place she sometimes visited. That place no one else could see.

Aunt Charlotte stopped spinning and stood up. She walked to the table and laid her hand on Momma's shoulder. "No, Miss Miller. My sister has no other children. Now, Ellie, she has two more brothers, and you will get them in the school when they turn six." Aunt Charlotte squeezed momma's shoulder and walked back over to the spinning wheel. She sat down and started spinning again without speaking another word.

"Two weeks, you say?" Suddenly Momma was herself again. "That'll give me just enough time to make some proper school clothing for Titus. And shoes. He'll surely need shoes. He's been running around barefoot all summer."

Miss Miller nodded and sipped the lemonade. Sweat beads gathered on her forehead, just like those Titus felt on his own face. She took a white handkerchief from the pocket of her brown skirt and blotted the moisture from her face. She stood then, turning towards the door. Titus was surprised to see that her shoes were old and dusty. The white women he had seen before usually had prettier shoes.

She walked away from the table and spoke to Titus once again. "I will look forward to seeing you at school in two weeks, Titus. Just up the road, your neighbors the Shepards will be sending their two children, Ruth and Raymond, to school. I expect you can walk with them, and they can show you the way until you meet up with your cousin at the bottom of the hill. Then you can all walk together, along with the other children from the village." With that, the special visitor walked out the door and down the path to the road.

Chapter 2

September 11, 1864

Titus burst out the door of the Free Will Baptist Church and ran ahead of Momma and Poppa to catch up with Ellie. "I can't wait, Ellie; school starts tomorrow. Momma's been sewing all week, and yesterday at Dunham's I got new shoes."

"Took a lot of butter churning to trade for those shoes, Titus King. You best take care and not wear them to the barn."

"Stop bossing me, Ellie Peters. I know how to take care of my shoes."

"Come along, Son, we have chores to get to before the sun drops behind the hill." Poppa strode up from behind and laid a hand on Titus's shoulder. The families parted ways at the bottom of the hill, and Titus asked his poppa for a shoulder ride to the top. Some days, Poppa was too tired, but on church day he usually hoisted Titus high into the air for the long walk up the steep hill to their house. Sure enough, today was no different, and soon Titus was settled into his favorite perch on Poppa's strong broad shoulders, high enough to see the tops of the trees with their new fall colors sparkling in the late afternoon sun.

"Poppa, aren't those trees a sight? Ellie says Miss Miller has special coloring sticks at school and we can make pictures there. I want to make a picture of the trees on the hill. Do you think I can do that, Poppa?" Titus continued chattering nonstop to Poppa and Momma all the way up the hill. Sunday was his favorite day of the week. Both Poppa and Momma put on their finest clothes and came down the hill to go to church. They didn't spend the whole day working, and after church when they walked home Titus had them all to himself. No cows or sheep and no other grown folk. Just their little family and the trees and flowers and squirrels.

Poppa laughed a lot on these walks, that deep laugh rising up from his belly and making his whole body shake. And sometimes they sang altogether while they were walking. Poppa's favorite song, which he'd just started to sing, was "My Darling Nellie Gray," an old song he learned while he was in Philadelphia after he escaped from Virginia. Riding on Poppa's shoulders and singing out those words made him feel like a true king, not just a little boy with the name of Titus King.

~~

Titus walked into the house just after Poppa when they finished their chores. Poppa started lighting the oil lamp; Momma already had lit the smaller lamp on the kitchen stand. She sat in the small circle of light, sewing a button on a shirt.

"Is that my school shirt, Momma?"

"Yes, Titus, this is the last thing I have to sew, and then you are all ready for school. I already set your lunch pail in the icebox. I fixed you three biscuits with jam and a jar of fresh milk."

"A whole jar of milk?" Titus threw his arms around his momma's neck, nearly knocking the needle and thread from her hands. "Oh, Momma, thank you! I will be the richest boy at school with my own jar of milk. Did you and Poppa take a lunch pail when you went to school in Virginia?"

"Your Poppa and I, we never went to school, Titus. You will be the first in this line of the King family to go to school."

Poppa set the oil lamp on its stand and came to sit by Momma and Titus. "That's right, Son. Remember, your momma and I, we were slaves in Virginia. Slaves didn't have no schools. Slaves were never allowed to read words or learn to do math sums."

Titus could hardly believe what he was hearing. His poppa was the smartest man he knew. How did he get so smart if he never went to school? "Poppa, I seen you do your math sums when we take the butter to Dunham's store. You know your numbers. I seen you do it."

Poppa laughed and his belly started to shake a little. "You are right about that, Son. I learned my numbers right quick when we got to Vermont. Need to know how to do numbers if you ain't going to be cheated when you have money and goods to manage. My Clark kinfolk saw to it that I learned my numbers soon as I got up here. But reading— naw, I never did learn to read."

"Your poppa almost learned to read one time when he was not much bigger than you." Momma said, winking at Poppa, "Tell Titus the story, Harris. Go on now, the boy is heading to school; he should hear that story."

Poppa took a deep breath and let it out real slow. His long fingers tapped a soft rhythm on the table, and the rest of the house was quiet. Titus waited. He loved when his poppa told old stories about the Virginia farm. They were scary sometimes, but Poppa always made them happy in the end, and sometimes Titus fell asleep listening to Poppa's deep, soft voice.

The tapping stopped. Poppa laid both hands across his knees, tipped his head back and closed his eyes. His lips began moving, but no sound was coming out. Titus waited. Momma finished her sewing and stood to put her needle and thread back in the case above the kitchen sink.

Poppa opened his eyes and took another deep breath, letting it out even more slowly this time. "Long, long time ago, Titus, I was a boy no bigger than you."

"And you lived on a farm with a big house."

"That's right, son. I lived on the farm with the big house. Most of my kinfolk, my momma and pappie and all my brothers and sisters, they worked out in the fields. But I got picked to work in the milk house. I liked it there, milking the cows. I felt safe and the sun didn't beat on my back like it did on the others. The only problem, the master's little girl, Miss Bonnie, she sometimes came in the milk house and watched me work. My momma warned me not to talk to her. She told me terrible things would happen, and I might even be sold if I talked to her."

"Did you talk to her, Poppa? Did terrible things happen to you?"

Poppa laughed. "You wait a bit, Titus; you are jumping ahead of the story. No, I didn't talk to her at first. I just milked the cows quietly. Sometimes I talked to the cows, but never to Miss Bonnie." Poppa stopped talking and lifted his hands from his knees. He began tapping his fingers on the table again.

"Until that one day, Harris. Go on, the boy needs to hear the whole story."

"Were you there too, Momma?"

"No Titus, I wasn't even born yet when this story happened. But I have heard it many a time. Go on now, Harris, finish the story."

"Miss Bonnie, she would sit on a bale of hay by the barn door. She had a book on her lap every day. She called it a primer. She'd practice her reading. Every day she would sit there and read. I felt an ache in me something fierce, Titus. I knew I wanted to read like her one day, but I was too scared to listen, afraid I would learn some words and I might be killed for it."

"Killed for words?" Titus could hardly believe what he was hearing.

"Yes, Son. The slaves knew that learning to read words on paper could get you killed. The master had no patience for uppity slaves. Reading and writing, you see, that was only for the white folk. It was beat into us that reading was a dangerous thing. Dangerous." Poppa's eyes grew large, and Titus shivered, waiting for the good part of the story. Poppa never told a story without a good part.

Titus didn't notice Momma moving about, but all at once she was standing next to Poppa with a drinking glass. Poppa took a deep, long drink and then a deep, long breath, and then he started in on the story again.

"Reading was dangerous, but it was also something we dreamed about. Learning to read was important if we wanted freedom. My pappie, he told us one day we would have freedom, and then all the children would go to school just like the white children, and we would read, and we would be free. I wanted to read those words in Miss Bonnie's book, Titus. I wanted to read those words so badly I could almost taste the letters moving across my tongue."

"So your Poppa, he became brave and foolish all at the same time one day." Momma said.

"Yes. True, Nan King, true indeed. Brave and foolish." Poppa shook his big head and laughed again."

"What happened?" Titus asked, moving his chair a little closer to Poppa.

"Miss Bonnie, I think she could read more than her little primer book. I think she could read my mind. She started asking me each day, 'Do you want to learn to read, Harris King?' and each day I told her, 'No, Miss Bonnie. No, thank you. Slaves can't learn to read.' I said it just like that every day until one day she asked again and I said, 'Do you think you could teach me just a little bit?'"

Titus gasped. "Did she do it? Did she teach you, Poppa?"

"She said, 'Come over here, Harris. Sit next to me, and I will teach you to read.' I finished with the cow, and I walked right over to her. Brave and foolish. I sat down on the hay bale, right beside her." He shook his head from side to side. Momma poked him in the ribs.

"Just then, the master came in. He saw me sitting next to his daughter and flew into a rage. He sent her into the big house, and next thing I know I was getting the worst whipping of my life. I really thought I was going to die, right in that barn with those cows as my only witnesses, Titus. I didn't want the master to hear me cry, so I bit down on my tongue until I could taste blood inside my mouth. At the same time, I saw big drops of blood from my back dripping onto the straw beneath my feet. I feared for my life, Titus, I was mighty a'feared. I started singing 'John Saw the Number' inside my head, but still didn't let a sound sneak past my lips."

Titus felt wet tears sliding down his cheeks. He got up from his chair and scampered over to his momma. She lifted him to her lap, and he turned his face into her chest. He wanted Poppa to go on, but he didn't know if he could bear to hear any more of this story.

After several quiet moments, Poppa began to speak again, "They sold me after that. Master said I could not be trusted near his daughter, Miss Bonnie. Sold me away from my momma and pappie and everyone I knew. I had to sleep on a little mat on the floor of a cabin in the slave quarters at a new master's plantation. I didn't know anybody there, and this time I had to work in the fields, not in the milk house."

"Poppa, your stories always have a good part, but there is no good part to this story."

"Oh, that's not quite true, Son. Your Poppa didn't tell you the good part yet. Go on Harris; tell the boy the end of the story so he can go to bed. He starts school tomorrow morning, and he needs his sleep. Our boy Titus, he's going to learn to read. And no one will beat him or sell him off. It's a miracle, Harris. An answer to many years of prayer."

"Your momma is right, Titus. It is fully dark now. Your belly is full and your chores are finished. It's time for bed, young fellow."

"But Poppa, I need to hear the good part of the story."

Poppa stood up and lifted Titus out of his mother's lap. He carried him to his bed and laid him down, pulling the quilt covers up around his shoulders. "The good part. Ah yes. You see, Titus, I didn't know anyone when I started at that new plantation. But there was a family there, a slave family that was kind to me and took care of me. And after a few years, they had a new baby girl. And that pretty little baby girl, well she grew up to be your momma. I would never have met your momma if my first master never did sell me that day. And you, my son, would never have been born. That's not just the good part. That's the best part."

Titus' eyelids were so heavy he couldn't keep them open to see Poppa's face. But he could feel him smiling, so Titus smiled too, and fell into a deep, hard sleep.

Chapter 3

October 18, 1864

Titus felt the cold wind against his back as he walked home from school with Ellie, Ruth, and Raymond. The bright blue-sky days of fall were starting to get cooler late in the day, and by the time they left the schoolhouse there was a definite chill in the air. Perfect air for pumpkins and apples to grow, Miss Miller told them. Today, she had allowed each pupil to gather apples that had fallen from the trees in the schoolyard to take home in their lunch pails. Titus was excited to show Momma the five shiny red apples in his pail. Maybe she would make another pie like the one they had on Sunday when the Pastor of the Free Will Baptist Church had come to their house for supper. But the walk home was long, and with the apples the pail was heavier than usual. Titus was tempted to eat just one along the way. He set his pail down and looked in to find the shiniest apple of them all.

"What are you doing Titus King?" No sooner had the pail settled onto the dirt road than Ellie peered over his shoulder ready to give Titus a piece of her mind.

"I'm fixin' to eat an apple. It's been a long while since lunch, and I'm hungry. And the pail is heavy."

"Good idea, Titus, I think I will have one too," Raymond said, finding a level spot in the road near Titus to set his pail down as well.

Ellie and Ruth looked at each other. Ruth shrugged her shoulders and almost set her pail down too, when Ellie stomped her foot soundly on the road. "No!" She yelled at the other three children.

Not wanting to be bossed by Ellie, Titus quickly snatched the largest apple from his pail and sank his teeth into it. With a full mouth, he mumbled, "You can't tell me what to do, Ellie Peters."

Ruth and Raymond both gasped.

Ellie shook her finger in front of Titus' face. "Don't you remember nothing from that letter Miss Miller read to us? Perhaps Raymond and Ruth can afford to eat an apple, Titus King, but you know very well we cannot do so."

Ruth straightened up, clutching her lunch pail to her side. "We won't eat any, Ellie. I was thinking about that letter too. It ain't right for those soldiers not to git enough food. My momma is going to help your family prepare packages to send down to South Carolina for your men."

"She is?" Ellie narrowed her eyes.

"Yes, it's true, Ellie. I heard her talking about it with our poppa last night at supper. Some of the other families from the First Congregational Church are going to make packages too," Raymond added.

Titus felt ashamed. He looked at the apple in his hand and suddenly it didn't look so shiny anymore. He stopped chewing and looked from Ellie to Ruth. From Ruth to Raymond. From Raymond back to Ellie. He felt trapped. He didn't know what to do.

"Titus, why don't you share that apple with Raymond since you done bit out of it already. And I'll put one of my apples in your pail so you will still have five." Ruth was always trying to make peace in the schoolyard, and now she was doing it here too. She reached into her pail and plucked out a large, shiny McIntosh apple, nestling it gently into Titus's pail so as not to bruise it.

"That was nice of you and all, Ruth, but he's still getting his behind whipped when I tell Uncle Harris what he did."

"You are not walking all the way up the hill just to tell your Uncle

Harris about an apple, Ellie. You go ahead to your house. We'll finish getting Titus home like we do every day." Ruth's words settled the discussion, and soon they reached the bottom of the hill where Ellie turned to go to her own house.

"You best not eat any more of those apples Titus King," she called over her shoulder as she skipped down the path to her house where her two little brothers played with a stick and ball in the front yard.

"Do you think it's true, what that letter said?" Raymond asked his sister. Titus leaned closer so he could hear her answer.

"Of course it's true, Raymond. Miss Miller would never read us something that wasn't true. She's a teacher. Teachers always tell the truth. That's why I want to be a teacher someday when I'm grown."

"But if you're a teacher you can't git a husband," Raymond said.

"Who needs a husband? I got brothers. That's all the menfolk I expect to need."

~~

Three other women from the Clark farm were in the kitchen with Momma when Titus walked through the door. Buckets and buckets filled with apples covered every inch of the floor. The women were peeling and cutting the apples, and Miss Lucy was stirring a big pot on top of the stove.

Titus wasn't surprised to see this. Ever since the letter from Loudon Langley reached the hill community, the women were working harder and harder to prepare packages of food, blankets, bandages, and other needed items to send to the colored soldiers serving in the Massachusetts 54th. Miss Miller had even read one of the letters at school, the one that

50

had been published in the Burlington Free Press telling how the colored soldiers didn't get as much food or supplies as the white soldiers.

"Momma, I brought home some apples in my lunch pail, see? Can you send these apples to the soldiers too? Maybe Ellie's poppa, Uncle William, would like an apple pie."

"Titus, how did you get those apples? Did you trade away your lunch? Whose farm did you get them from?" A look of fear spread across Momma's face as the other women all stopped working and stared at Titus, waiting for his answer.

"No, Momma; Miss Miller let all of us gather up apples from the schoolyard after we finished our lunch. Everyone got apples. Ellie got some too. And Ruth and Raymond."

A smile spread across Momma's face. "That's wonderful son. We were short a few apples, weren't we, sisters?"

The other women all nodded, and one of them said, "We sure were. I think we needed at least four or maybe five more to finish our work, How many do you have young man?"

"I have five," Titus said proudly, bringing the pail to his momma. She lifted the apples out one at a time, shining each one on her apron before passing it to Aunt Lydia for peeling and cutting.

"Here's some milk and a biscuit for you, Titus. Now sit down and tell us what you learned in school today, and then you can change your clothes and go down to the barn to help Poppa finish with the sheep and cows."

"We practiced reading. The other new pupils and me, we're almost finished with our first primer. Miss Miller showed us the new books we will start after Christmas. The new books have many rhymes and stories." Titus took a big bite of biscuit and washed it down noisily with a swallow of fresh, warm milk.

Miss Lucy was still stirring the pot on the cook stove, but she turned her head towards the other women and said, "Nan King, you must be so grateful to finally have a child live long enough to go to school."

Titus felt his back grow stiff. He looked at Momma waiting to see what would happen. He hoped she would not stare hard at the ceiling and go to that faraway place she sometimes visited whenever someone talked about her other children.

"Lucy Clark, you know Harris and I have two girls that are close to full grown by now. Lil'Bet and Sal; why, they might have been schooled, somewhere. Maybe they made it to Philadelphia or Ohio or even Canada before the war. Or maybe they got freed after the Emancipation Proclamation. I pray every day my girls are living and breathing and reading and writing, just like the master's children."

This time, Momma didn't go to her faraway place, but her eyes got all sparkly, almost like bits of fire would shoot right out of them over to Miss Lucy. Titus held his breath and set his milk glass on the table. Momma almost never talked about the two older sisters he never met. When Poppa and Momma were still slaves in Virginia, they had two little girls, Lil'Bet and Sal. One day their master sold the girls away to another master. Poor Momma never saw her daughters again.

Titus remembered that was the very day when Poppa made the plan to escape. They waited and waited for the weather to get cold and the crops to be harvested. Then on the darkest night of the month of November of 1854, they ran for their lives. They heard there was a man by the name of William Still in Philadelphia who would help them start a new life of freedom. And they knew they had family way up north in a place called Vermont. It took them two years to make it to the hill in

Vermont. While they were in Philadelphia, they had a baby boy, Benjamin, but Momma was so weak from running away from Virginia, baby Benjamin died before he reached his first birthday. Titus never got to meet him, either.

Titus had heard the story of Momma and Poppa's brave escape to Philadelphia, and their journey through New Jersey and Connecticut to Vermont many times. It was filled with daring adventures of swimming across rivers, shivering in barn lofts waiting for slave hunters and their dogs to pass, and wrapping their bleeding feet in leaves from the trees so they could go on one more day. Every time Poppa told the story, he added new parts Titus had never heard, but one thing he never did—he never mentioned the names of Lil'Bet, Sal, or Benjamin.

Two more baby boys had been born here in Vermont, but Josiah and Samuel didn't live long at all. They were both buried in the Clark family burial ground at the top of the hill. Sometimes Momma went up there and just sat all day, silent, in her faraway place. When Titus was born, no one expected him to live very long either. The whole hill community thought Harris and Nan King were cursed to a life with no children.

But Titus lived.

And now, he was learning to read.

Momma stood up and pulled an old Bible from the shelf by the fireplace. "Read me some words, Titus. Read some words for all of us."

Titus didn't know how to read many of the hard words in the Bible yet. Most of these words were not in the school primer. But he knew how to find the page with his name on it. The Book of Titus. And he knew how to read one part, "To Titus, mine own son."

All of the women stopped working on the apples and clapped their hands. Even Miss Lucy. Titus felt warm and happy. He ran to give his

Momma a hug. Tears were on her face, but she was smiling.

"Scram now, Titus. Surely Poppa needs your help in the barn." She said, pushing him away. Titus picked up his milk glass, gulped down the last of the warm liquid, and ran out the door.

Chapter 4

December 23, 1864

The brutal winds whistled through the schoolhouse walls as if they weren't there. Titus could see his own breath, and his hands and feet were nearly numb. If it was this cold inside, what would it be like for the walk home? His school shoes were no match for the snow and ice, but there was no money for a pair of boots yet this year. "At least I have the hat and scarf Momma knit for me," he said to himself. He longed to go warm his hands by the wood burning stove at the front of the classroom, but the older white boys were up there, and he knew if he approached them he'd get pushed right back to his seat.

Miss Miller stood at the front of the room clapping her hands and instructing all the pupils to take their seats. The five boys by the woodstove were the last to sit. "Students, students, we have only a short time left before our Christmas break begins. The next time I see you it will be a new year. Eighteen hundred and sixty five! Before I dismiss you, I have a surprise for the first grade pupils today. When I call your name, please come to the front of the classroom and bring your primer with you. Raymond Shepard. Thomas Ballard. Josephine Crosby. Titus King."

Titus was surprised to be called to the front of the classroom. He and the other three small first graders scampered up to the front and huddled near the woodstove. He glanced up and saw his cousin Ellie smiling from ear to ear. Ruth Shepard smiled too. *They must know what this is about*, Titus thought.

Miss Miller walked from one student to the next, checking to see that they had their primers in hand. "I am very proud of my first grade pupils. You have worked very hard to learn your letters and to read from our little first primer. Today, as part of our Christmas celebration, I will ask each of you to read one page aloud to the class. If you are able to read your page without stumbling, you will be allowed to keep your primer. Take it home, read it to your younger brothers and sisters. Use it for practice. When you return to school in January, you will receive a new book. A much harder book. You will begin using the New England Primer along with the second and third grade pupils."

Titus' heart was pounding so loud he could hardly hear Miss Miller. All he could think about was bringing home the primer. Poppa would be so happy. Momma might even cry. He could show them all the reading he had learned. He remembered the day in September when he told them how excited he was to learn that each letter of the alphabet had a sound. Now he could show them how the sounds come together to make words. What a happy day! But first, first he had to read a page in front of the whole class. The colored students and the white students. His cousins and friends. The mean big boys. And Miss Miller.

"Titus? Titus, can you hear me?" Miss Miller's voice sounded funny, like she had cotton in her mouth. Why was she talking like that?

"Yes, Miss Miller," he heard himself say. The words came out of his mouth but they sounded funny too. He suddenly felt very hot, and he was afraid he was going to fall to the floor. Maybe he was standing too close to the woodstove. He stepped away. His feet were still frozen. How could his face be so hot while his feet were still frozen?

"Titus, it is your turn. If you would like to take your primer home, I need you to turn to page nineteen and read it to the class."

"Yes Miss Miller." Titus opened his primer, turning pages until he came to page nineteen. Two boys in funny clothes and hats perched on a fence. A bird was in the air by their heads. A puppy with his nose in the air stood guard by their feet. Under the picture were words. So many words.

"Titus?" Miss Miller said his name again. Titus looked up at her and gulped. "Read the words on the page, Titus."

Titus wiggled his tingling fingers. They had been frozen and now they were waking up. It felt like a hundred of Momma's sewing needles were stabbing the tips of each finger. His ears were burning. All the eyes in the classroom were on him.

"'These boys have found a bird's nest.'" Titus started to read. He was doing it. The letters were forming words. The words were coming together on his tongue. He was saying the words out loud. *I can do this,* he thought, continuing. "'See the young birds.'" Soon Titus had finished reading the whole page. Miss Miller clapped. Everyone was clapping. Something was doing flip-flops inside his stomach. His fingers were still tingling, and now his toes were tingling too.

"Good job, Titus King. You may keep your primer and take it home. Be sure to write your name on the inside. It is yours, now. Raymond Shepard, please turn to page twenty-seven. It is your turn to read."

Titus held his breath and looked at his friend, wondering if Raymond felt as scared as he did. Raymond didn't look scared. He stood straight and tall. He turned the pages in his primer and then began to read, "Grandfather has come to see the girls and boy." Titus let his breath out slowly. Raymond did it too. Now they would both have primers to bring home. What a happy day.

~~

The wind had picked up. The snow was crunchy and deep. Icicles hung from every tree branch. Puffy white breath-clouds encircled the four children as they walked home from school for the last time before Christmas. Titus held tightly to his primer, so filled with happy pride that he did not complain about the deep cold setting into his bones.

"I was so proud of both of you," Ellie said. "You did the best. Better than Thomas or Josephine."

"That's not charitable, Ellie. I was proud of our brothers too, but Thomas and Josephine did a good job."

"Oh, Ruth, do you have to be so nice all the time?"

"Well of course, Ellie, especially at Christmas. Don't you want to be nice at Christmas? I hope you have presents to give you momma, so she won't feel so sad about your poppa being far away in the war."

"We are not having presents in our house this year." Ellie said. "Momma says all our efforts have to go to the men in the war."

"But it's Christmas, Ellie; surely you can think of something to make your momma smile. What about you, Titus? Do you have a present for your Momma and Poppa?"

"No, Ruth, I don't. We've been making packages for the soldiers. We didn't have no time to make presents for anyone around here."

"I can't believe a Christmas with no presents," Raymond said. "Everyone has to have a present on Christmas. God even says so."

"What are you giving your parents, Ruth?" Ellie asked.

"Poppa let me keep three pounds of butter last week. He let me trade it at Dunham's myself so I picked out a comb for Momma and a pair of socks for Poppa. I picked out something for Raymond too, but I can't talk about it right now."

"That sounds just right. I'm sure they'll be happy when they open those gifts. You'll have a very blessed Christmas at your house. I'm going to try to come up with some idea. Something to give my Momma and my two little brothers. I have two days to do something. You'll see, we'll have a blessed Christmas too."

"Yes, Ellie, I'm sure you will," Ruth replied.

Titus listened to the whole conversation with his head down. He had been so happy about the primer, but now he felt sad. He had nothing to give Momma and Poppa. Nothing at all. He pulled his hat down over his ears. He was feeling colder and colder with every step towards home.

Chapter 5

December 25, 1864

Titus stared at the ceiling, willing a thread of light to slip through the window shutters. "Come, Christmas, come. Come, baby Jesus, wake up the sun. I can't wait. I can't wait." Titus whispered aloud over and over. At last, the tiniest sliver of light slid into the room. Morning at last! Titus threw off his covers and ran to Momma and Poppa's bed. "Wake up! Wake up! It's Christmas!" he said, shaking Momma's shoulders and bouncing on the bed until they opened their eyes. "It's Christmas, It's Christmas!" he repeated.

Titus smiled to himself remembering his strange behavior over the last two days. After the conversation on the way home from school with Ellie, Ruth, and Raymond, Titus had worried and worried over what to give Momma and Poppa for Christmas. He had trudged in silence up the hill towards his house, not hearing the rest of the things that Ruth and Raymond chattered about after Ellie turned to her own house at the bottom of the hill. Just seconds before they reached his house the perfect idea came to him. He had been bursting with excitement ever since, hardly able to stop himself from spilling the secret until this morning. He was so agitated Poppa said he had ants in his pants, and Momma was worried he might have a fever. Now, Christmas morning was finally here and he could not wait one more minute.

"Get up! Get up!"

"Titus King, Happy Christmas to you, Son. Now settle down a bit; the dawn isn't even fully broke yet. We have a good while before we head down the hill for Christmas Day services." Poppa tried to close his eyes again, but Titus jumped on him.

"Please Poppa, get up, get up. It's Christmas morning, and I have a big surprise for you and Momma."

Poppa sat up and took a big breath. He swung his long legs out of bed and plunked his heavy flat feet onto the floor. "Oh, all right now, Titus. Let me git the fire rekindled so we don't freeze to death." Poppa stood and walked toward the fire. Soon, he was singing, "Wasn't that a Mighty Day" in his croaky morning voice.

Momma sat up and surprised Titus by snatching him into a big bear hug. "Happy Christmas, Son. May God bless our family for another year."

As soon as Momma let go of him, Titus began dancing around the house, singing along with Poppa, who had moved on from "Mighty Day" to "Go Tell It on the Mountain."

"I'm telling you, Nan, our boy has ants in his pants."

Momma laughed. "He has 'Christmas fever' is all." She bent on her knees and pulled a package wrapped in newsprint from under the bed and held it on her lap as she sat down on the sofa, pulling a quilt across her shoulders. "We have a surprise for you too, Titus."

"Sit down, Poppa, so I can give you both the surprise," Titus said.

"Why don't you open yer present first, Son, while I put the coffee on the stove to boil?"

Momma handed Titus the package. Titus dropped to his knees on the floor by her feet and tore the newsprint off. Underneath was a brand new pair of winter boots. Titus sprang to his feet and gave his momma a bear hug. "Thank you Momma; thank you Poppa," he said, clutching the new boots close to his chest.

"We know it gets mighty cold walking up and down that hill to school all winter. It's not a toy or plaything, but I hope you like it," Momma said.

"Oh, yes, I do, and now Miss Miller will let me play outside in the snow at lunch time. She only lets pupils with boots and coats outdoors to play, Momma. Thank you. I can't wait to go outside in the snow." Titus sat on the floor and began wiggling the boots on over his heavy woolen socks. For a moment, he forgot about the surprise for his parents.

Poppa finished fixing the coffee and came to sit on the sofa next to Momma. Titus had both boots on and stood to stamp his feet fully into them. And then he remembered.

"Momma, Poppa, it's my turn. Close your eyes." Titus waited to be sure they both had their eyes firmly closed and then reached under his bed for the small package wrapped in a scrap of cloth he'd found in Momma's sewing basket. He tiptoed to the sofa and gently laid the package on Poppa's knees.

"Open your eyes!"

Momma and Poppa looked at the package and then looked at Titus.

"Go ahead," he said, "Open it up."

Together, his parents pulled the cloth off to reveal the present underneath. They stared at the small book; Momma opened it to the first page and saw where Titus had written his name.

"It's my primer!" Titus danced and hopped on one foot and then the other. Then, he let the words he'd been holding in for two days tumble out like water from a spigot. "All the first grade pupils had to stand in front of the class and read a page. Miss Miller said if we could read it, we could take the primer home, and it would be ours to keep. I did it. I read page nineteen in front of the whole class, and Miss Miller said I could keep the primer. I get a new one in January."

Momma was beaming at him. Poppa had barely drawn a breath. He was running his hands over the cover of the primer again and again.

"Read us that page, Titus. Read us page nineteen," Momma said.

Titus turned to page nineteen and read the very words he read at school two days earlier. "'See the young birds,'" he read. Momma had tears on her cheeks.

"I didn't know what I could give you for Christmas. I thought I didn't have anything to give you, but then I remembered that story about Miss Bonnie and the primer and the milk barn and how badly you wanted to learn to read words, Poppa. So I am giving you my primer, and I can read it with you, and I can show you how the letters make sounds. And how the sounds go together to make words. I can show you, Poppa, and you can learn to read, and no one will whip you for it, Poppa. You can read, and it won't be dangerous."

Poppa had tears on his cheeks now too. "That's the good part of the story, Titus," he said.

"No Poppa, it's not just the good part. It's the best part!"

3 UMOJA

Chapter 1

December 25

Tires crunched on the thin layer of snow as they turned into the driveway. Clearly it had been shoveled once already. Celia Evers guessed Billy had tackled it while they were gone. She stepped gingerly out of the car to avoid slipping on the slick surface, wearing only dress shoes and not snow boots. Breathing in the crisp air, she stood admiring the beauty around her. Snow-laden evergreen branches bowed closer to the driveway. Twigs, small stones, and lampposts glimmered in their fresh white coats. Soft flakes still swirling from above glittered in front of the living room window, catching the colors from the Christmas tree lights inside and forming dozens of mini-fireworks displays cascading to the lawn below.

"Gotcha!"

Celia's reverie came to an abrupt close as the remnants of a softly packed snowball smacked her chin, breaking apart and sending tiny ice-shards down her neck and into the front of her party dress. Homer was already packing another snowball.

Celia ducked in time to avoid the second missile headed her way and scooped up a handful of snow to toss back in his direction. "You're asking for it now," she exclaimed, rushing him and thrusting a handful of fresh snow down the back of his shirt. Giggling like high-school students, the two romped in the snow for several minutes before the numbness in their hands and feet drove them inside.

Stomping her feet on the rug inside the door, Celia was not surprised that no one looked up. It was Christmas night, after all, and she imagined that all six children would be fixated on their favorite gifts. Celia looked around the room as she slipped off her shoes and slid her feet into the new slippers Jackie had given her that morning.

As expected, CJ was playing in the entryway hall with his new remote control car. Sammy sat next to the fireplace, smiling in his wheelchair and listening to a CD through his comfy new headphones. Rocky was curled up in a corner of the couch reading her new book. Billy was the exception. He wasn't busy with any gifts, but rather sprawled across a living room chair sound asleep and snoring, his lanky six-foot frame not looking terribly comfortable with limbs shooting out in all directions. Only Dev and Jackie were not immediately visible. Celia guessed that Dev was ensconced in his room trying out his new computer apps.

Jackie burst into the living room wearing an apron over her PJs and a dusting of flour up to her elbows. "I'm glad you're home, you know? I think the turkey is finished, but I need dad to check it, okay?" Celia had missed her daughter's unique sing-songy voice, turning every sentence into a question, while the teen was away for her first semester of college.

It was nice to have her home for the holidays.

"I'll take a look. It sure smells good, Jackster," Homer said, hanging his jacket on the hall coat tree and shaking snow out of his hair.

"Thanks so much for taking charge of Christmas dinner so we could enjoy ourselves at the wedding. Did you make rolls too? Is that why you're covered with flour?" Celia asked. Both she and Homer followed Jackie as a symphony of aromas including rosemary, sage, cinnamon, nutmeg, and mint lured them to the kitchen.

"Oh my word, Jackie, did you call the fire department when the bomb went off in here?"

"Funny, Dad. I'm not used to fixing a whole meal by myself, you know? I didn't want to bug the kids to help me. They love playing with their new toys, right? And I kind of like just listening to my music and, you know, thinking about stuff."

Celia surveyed the room. It did look a little like a war zone. Thankfully-- there didn't appear to be any casualties. A basket of fresh rolls sat on the counter next to a large pot of mashed potatoes. The beginnings of a salad were strewn across the cutting-board surface on the center island. The item that stopped her in her tracks was the large ceramic cookie platter piled high with perfectly golden shortbread cookies. "You made the cookies," she managed to say, trying not to cry.

"Duh; of course I did, Mom. It wouldn't be Christmas without Nanna's shortbread cookies, would it?"

"I can't believe you did this all by yourself. I'm so, so . . . I'm just so . . . "

"Ah—speechless, I guess? Wow, that's a first."

"Good one, Jackie," Homer said, pulling on oven mitts, "and your mom is right, this is pretty awesome. Let me check this turkey, and we'll call everyone to the table."

"Let's finish putting this salad together while dad carves the turkey. And you can tell me what you meant when you said you were 'thinking about stuff.' Is there something on your mind you want to talk about?" Celia began chopping red bell peppers, avoiding eye contact, knowing that Jackie found it easier to talk when she didn't have to also look.

"Well, first I was just thinking how nice it is to be back home. I know you can't believe it, but I missed you all when I was at school. Even the rug rats. Crazy, right? And, well, you know? I love our family traditions. When I was moving from home to home in foster care, I never really knew where I would be for Christmas? So there was no tradition. And when I was at college, I knew I'd come home and we'd do all the same stuff we do every year, like when we get to open one present on Christmas Eve after church? And you always pretend you don't know what's in it?" Jackie suddenly swept Celia into a rare hug, transferring flour all over Celia's fancy dress. And totally worth it. As Jackie released her mom, she switched gears, asking, "So, how was the wedding?"

Celia tossed the diced peppers into the salad bowl and started chopping a tomato. She described Tina and Brent's wedding to her daughter, painting a picture of the magic created by hearing them say their vows outside in the gently falling snow. Tina had been through so much loss and disappointment in recent years, and then a special lunch with a new friend from church a few months back changed the direction of her life. She regained her faith, found new friends, a new job, and a romance that led to marriage. Since it all started with lunch at Deanie's Diner, Tina had invited the entire staff, including Homer, to the wedding.

Celia was delighted to share the occasion with Tina and Brent, even if it meant giving up her traditional Christmas afternoon nap. But it was also good to be back at home, resuming the traditions that had helped to knit this motley crew into a fiercely bonded family. After the wild, intense, and bustling activities of Christmas Eve and morning, she was glad that Christmas dinner was always a comfy-casual affair in the Evers house. No one even changed out of their PJs.

"I'm going to send Rocky in to help you carry the food to the table while I slip back into my PJs," Celia said. "I just can't imagine eating Christmas dinner in this fancy-schmancy dress. And later, Jackie, you can tell me the rest of what's on your mind."

"How did you . . . ?" Jackie started to ask, but her mother had left the room.

"She reads your mind, Jackie. She reads mine too. Scary, sometimes, isn't it?" Celia smiled to herself as she heard Homer offer his explanation to Jackie.

~~

Celia and Jackie sat alone in the living room, bathed in the glow of the Christmas tree lights. Homer had gone upstairs to bathe Sammy and get him in bed. Everyone else had gone to their rooms except for Billy. He was in the kitchen washing the dishes.

"Billy's changed, mom. He would never volunteer to do dishes before he went to Juvie?"

"I think he gets more anxious now when he has free time. He doesn't quite know what to do with himself. He paces. And then he finds something to keep his hands and mind busy," Celia said.

"Yeah. That reminds me of what Vince told me when we had some of our talks at the campfires up at Loonstone Lake." Jackie said. She'd spent the summer working at a summer camp owned by family friends. While there, she met a young man who, like her brother Billy, had spent time in Juvie. "He said whenever he had free time he got scared that something bad would happen soon. It made me sad."

"It takes time to get past the impact of being locked up. It can be very traumatic. It makes me sad too, Jackster. But I hope and pray that Billy will make the adjustment in time. And your friend Vince too."

"Thanks, Mom." Jackie remained quiet for several moments. *It Came Upon A Midnight Clear* played softly in the background. Neither of them spoke. As the song changed to *God Rest Ye Merry Gentlemen,* Jackie shifted her position. "Speaking of Vince? He never called today. No text. Nothing. And when I tried to call him, you know? Just to say 'Merry Christmas?' I got one of those messages; his phone is turned off. I don't know what to think? The last time we talked he said he was going to try to come to Sweetland for Kwanzaa and New Year's. But now? I don't know."

Celia slipped her arm around her daughter's shoulders. "I don't know either, Jack, but our Kwanzaa celebration is still a few days away. I'm sure you'll hear something."

Jackie laid her head on her mom's shoulder and the two sat quietly listening to Christmas carols and watching the snow silently falling outside the window.

Chapter 2

December 26

Not a creature was stirring. Not even the proverbial mouse.

The precious silence didn't happen in the Evers household on the night *before* Christmas like it did in the famous story, but it finally arrived early on the morning *after* Christmas when exhausted children and teens were still snug in their beds longer than usual, and Celia and Homer could sit silently by the fireplace reflecting on the special moments of the last few days before launching into the busyness of planning and executing the remaining holiday festivities for Kwanzaa and New Year's Day.

"Ready for a slice of Panettone?" Celia asked. Five loaves of the special Christmas bread, made from a recipe handed down through several generations of Celia's family had been almost entirely devoured on Christmas morning; but as always, Celia had squirrelled away a couple of slices to share privately with Homer on the morning after. Very few things said 'home' and 'family' to Celia more than the redolent aroma of the toasted sweet bread, loaded with satiny chunks of citron and plump raisins and dotted with pads of quickly melting butter.

"You bet. I'll get the coffee."

Eating slowly to savor every morsel and every pleasure the morning had to offer, neither Celia nor Homer said a word. Oak logs crackled in the fireplace. Outside, the wind was picking up, creating a whistling sound across the top of the chimney and sending swirls of snow across the yard. The neighbor's dog barked at a passing car.

Reluctantly, Celia broke the spell. "It's eight o'clock. Sammy won't last much longer without breakfast."

Homer nodded, handed his empty cup to Celia, and rose to begin the morning routines. Celia took the two mugs to the kitchen and set them on the counter. She surveyed the scene. Billy had done a good job getting the dishes, pots, and pans washed, but the counters were still covered with a mash-up of flour, stray lettuce leaves, turkey bones, and assorted other reminders of last night's dinner. She filled the sink with hot soapy water and got to work.

A few minutes later, CJ bounded into the room. Relentlessly energetic, CJ never simply walked anywhere. Before Celia could stop him, he grabbed two cookies and popped one into his mouth.

"CJ! That's not breakfast," she scolded.

"I know. I'll eat breakfast too," he said with a crooked grin.

"Are you going to be my helper today? We have to shop for the food for our Kwanzaa meal today because I won't have any other time before Monday. And we can get the box of Kwanzaa decorations down here and set them up in the dining room."

"Yeah. Can we get more batteries when we go shopping? My remote control car died."

"Already? Did you wear a rut in the floor from playing with it so much?"

CJ started to walk toward the entryway hall, probably to check for grooves. He took everything so literally. Celia laughed, "CJ, I'm just kidding, I know there are no ruts. And I already have extra batteries upstairs in my room. I'll get you some when I go up to get dressed." Celia always made a point to have extra batteries on hand for the day after Christmas.

"Thanks, Mom. Can I ask you something?"

"Of course, what's up?"

"I love our Kwanzaa parties. Especially when Sophie and Bart come with their drums. Bart is really cool. Last time we went to the V-Inn for Rocky's birthday, Sophie was our waitress and she promised Bart would teach me to play those African drums."

"I like the drums too, and yes, Sophie and Bart are coming this year. Was that your question?" It was often hard to follow CJ's train of thought in conversations. With his ADHD, he was all over the place.

"Oh, no, I was just saying that. My question is about if it's okay for Christians to celebrate Kwanzaa?"

"Well of course it is, CJ, what made you wonder about that?"

"Mrs. Billings, my Sunday School teacher. I asked her if she wanted to come to our Kwanzaa party," he stopped, looking a little sheepish. "I hope you aren't mad."

"I'm not mad, CJ, but it is usually best to check with me or dad before you invite people over, okay? Anyhow, we'd love to have Mrs. Billings and her family come for Kwanzaa. What did she say?"

"She said no. But then she also said she was very disappointed to hear that we celebrated Kwanzaa. She said it was a 'devil's day' and not for Christians. What does that mean, a 'devil's day'?"

Celia finished scrubbing the last of the flour off the counter and dried her hands on a dishtowel. "Let's go get that box of Kwanzaa decorations and I can answer your question while we unpack them, okay?"

"Okay." CJ scampered ahead of her as they both moved towards the stairs to the second floor. On the way up, they passed Rocky and Billy coming down the stairs. Soon everyone would be up and the household would be buzzing.

"Good morning Rocky, Billy. There's plenty of fruit in the fridge, and there are still some cranberry-orange scones left if you want those. Or cereal. Billy—thanks for doing the cleanup last night. The clean dishes are still by the sink if you want to finish the job by putting them away this morning." Both kids grunted and continued down the stairs. Neither were great conversationalists, especially this early in the day.

After locating the Kwanzaa box in the storage room, Celia and CJ began unpacking it in the dining room. Lifting each individual item out of the box, Celia reviewed its meaning with CJ. As CJ placed the plastic vegetables on the woven straw mat, she said, "The vegetables remind us of the harvest, the crops grown by farmers who provide food for us. There are many languages in Africa, and in one of those languages, the word for crops is 'mazao.' Symbols of crops are part of the Kwanzaa celebration to remind us to give thanks for this year's harvest and to look forward with faith to next year's harvest. Does that remind you of anything from the Bible?"

"Ummmmm, I remember when it was Thanksgiving we had to memorize that verse about sowing seeds and harvesting crops. Is that the one you mean?" CJ asked.

"Yes, that's right – you memorized parts of Psalm 107 at Thanksgiving. And there are many other places in the Bible where God talks about being thankful for the harvest. So you see, this is one example of how the Kwanzaa celebration reminds us of important truths in our own faith. God created all people from all the lands of the world, and He gives each people and tribe different ways to celebrate and show his love."

"Cool." CJ was already moving on, picking up the candles to place in the *kinara*. "I remember this candle—it means *umoja*, right?"

"Good memory, CJ. And umoja means unity. It is one of the seven principles of Kwanzaa. And one of my favorite Bible verses—it's the one up there on the wall—can you read it to me?"

CJ stood and walked toward the couch, looking up at the words stenciled on the wall, "'Behold how good and pl-pl . . . ' what's that word?"

"Pleasant."

"'Behold how good and pleasant it is for brothers to dwell together in unity. Psalm 133:1'Oh now I remember—you made Billy and Dev read that one when they used to fight."

Celia laughed. "Bingo. It's a Kwanzaa principle, but it's also a Bible principle; and in this house it's an Evers principle. Maybe Mrs. Billings has just never understood Kwanzaa this way. Next time you have Sunday school you can share some of this with her. But for now go get dressed if you still want to come shopping with me."

~~

Celia and CJ pulled into the driveway just as the mail truck left. Celia instructed CJ to grab the mail out of the box while she hoisted two large grocery bags out of the back seat and headed into the house.

CJ deposited a stack of envelopes on the table. "More Christmas cards." He exclaimed, "Don't people know Christmas is over?"

"Christmas is never over, son." Homer said, walking into the room. "We celebrate the spirit of Christmas all year long. Now let's help unpack these groceries, okay?"

"Jackie!" Celia called out loudly, "You have some mail and I think you'll want it right away."

In a flash, Jackie bounded down the stairs and into the kitchen. Celia was holding a bright red envelope high in the air. Jackie tried to snatch it and Celia jumped away, eyes twinkling. "Come on, Mom, let me have it?"

After a few moments of teasing her daughter, Celia handed over the envelope and Jackie tore into it. "It's from Vince. He is coming for our Kwanzaa party, and he can stay for New Year's too? Oh Mom, you were right? There is a reason I didn't hear from him. He turned off his phone, you know? So he didn't have to pay the bill and he could save his money. For the bus ticket? He's coming Monday on the bus."

Celia smiled. She was nearly as excited as her daughter. After years of being the ice-princess, keeping all of her emotions bottled tightly inside her, this year Jackie had finally thawed a bit. This new, warmer young woman was a delight. They still butted heads at times, but that was starting to be outweighed by moments like this.

"Oh mom? I have so much to do. Rozene's wedding is tomorrow and I'm helping her decorate later today. She wants you to help too. I am so happy she is adopting my friends. From the group home? I can't believe she wanted me as a bridesmaid. No one ever wanted me like that before. Well, except you and Dad, of course."

"Rozene would not have her new family and your friends wouldn't have theirs if it hadn't been for you, Jackster. The day you asked Dad and me to get to know Wendy set the ball in motion for many lives to be changed. God used your kind heart to bring hope to so many people."

"I just can't wait to see all my friends tonight at the rehearsal. Wendy is coming too. I haven't seen her since graduation? We text all the time, but I worked all summer at camp and then went to college and never got to see her after the Dawkins adopted her. It hasn't been easy for her. Sometimes she wishes she still lived at the group home? But Mr.

and Mrs. Dawkins, they aren't giving up on her. Just like you and Dad never gave up on me."

"Yeah, and you were a real pain in the butt at times. You sure didn't make it easy on us," Celia said, only half joking.

Chapter 3

December 28

Sammy's cheeks were flushed red and warm to the touch. His eyes didn't have their usual life in them. He sat quiet and limp in his wheelchair. Celia prepared a cool washcloth to lay over his forehead as Homer spoke to her. "I don't think we should bring him out for church today, Cee. Don't want him to get worse. Someone will have to stay home."

"I agree. Jackie is staying home. When I woke her she announced to me that she wasn't going to church today."

"Announced?" Homer raised an eyebrow. "College girl thinks she's grown?"

"She's exhausted after yesterday's wedding festivities. She stayed up all night, I think, catching up with her friend Wendy. Plus she said she's had enough church this week," Celia replied, shaking her head and ticking off on her fingers, "Christmas Eve, Christmas Day, Rozene's wedding. She's churched-out."

"True story," Billy said, wandering into the kitchen. "I don't think I will go either. It snowed a little more last night. Me and Terrell want to get a jump on shoveling." He rubbed his fingers together indicating the cash he expected to make.

"I don't remember saying it was optional." Homer said.

"If Jackie can stay home, I shouldn't have to go. You can't force me."

"Son, let's not start the day like this. You have ninety minutes now before church. Go ahead and do some shoveling. Take my cell phone and call your mother a little before eleven and let us know where you are. We'll pick you up on the way to church. Terrell can come too."

Billy groaned, rolled his eyes, snatched the cell phone from his father, and then abruptly turned away. Walking towards the entryway, he began punching numbers on the phone keypad. "Yo, Terrell, you ready? Meet me at Fourth and Peach near Mrs. Smith's house. Maybe she'll let us shovel—she has that huge driveway. Then we can do the rest of that neighborhood. I have to quit at eleven—the 'rents are making me go to church. You can come with me and then we can go back out after, okay?"

Homer shook his head, "I don't know where his heart and mind will be at eleven, but at least I know his butt will be in church."

~~

Celia always enjoyed the service after Christmas. Between holiday travel, winter weather, and that 'churched-out' feeling some, like Jackie, had after the multiple holiday services, fewer people were in attendance. There was a warm, intimate, and personal atmosphere to the service. And it was a chance to enjoy some of her favorite music—less familiar carols that never made it into a service before Christmas like *In the Bleak Midwinter* and *I Wonder as I Wander.*

As soon as the pastor said the final benediction, Billy and Terrell bolted to resume their shoveling enterprise. Homer, Dev, and a few other dads and teens helped the youth group leader assemble a new air hockey table that had been donated to the group as a Christmas gift. CJ and Rocky were happily comparing notes about Christmas with their friends, so Celia poured herself a cup of coffee and mingled with the others in the fellowship parlor. All the chatter was about the many weddings in Sweetland this December—never had this small town had such a surge of romance during the holidays. Several church members had been in attendance at both Tina and Brent's wedding on Christmas Day, as well as Rozene and Mike's yesterday. While no one in this circle had been at the small ceremony earlier in the month uniting Dr. Bernard Thompson with the town matriarch, Virginia Livingston, people were still buzzing about that one as well.

"What a change in Virginia Livingston; you'd think she was an entirely different person." Zack Michaelson said.

"She's the poster child for that verse, 'Behold I make all things new,'" his wife Shellie added.

"Looks like you two don't get to be the newest newlyweds anymore. I heard Shellie's brother is thinking seriously about someone too. Another wedding on the horizon? How was your first holiday season as a married couple?" Celia asked.

"We may not be the town newlyweds anymore, but far as I'm concerned we're still on our honeymoon," Zack replied as Shellie blushed three shades of red. The small circle of folks gathered around the refreshment table laughed. "Nothing's certain about Will's proposition or lack thereof yet, though. You know Will."

~~

With lunch out of the way and everyone busy with their own activities, Celia brewed herself a cup of apple-cinnamon tea and picked up one of the new books she had received for Christmas. All the advance work for tomorrow's Kwanzaa party was finished, so it was a perfect afternoon for reading. She threw a large log on the fire so that it would last a long time, grabbed her favorite cozy lap blanket, and settled into her reading chair.

She was thoroughly enjoying the book and had halfway figured out the mystery when she heard her cell phone buzzing across the room from its perch on the charger. Debating whether to let it go to voice mail, she reluctantly got out of her chair, but by the time she reached the phone it had stopped. Caller ID indicated the call had come from Homer's phone. *Homer calling me? That's odd, he's upstairs.* Celia thought to herself. Just then the phone began buzzing again and she remembered that Billy had Homer's phone with him while shoveling. He was probably cold and asking for a ride home from some remote corner of town.

She picked up the phone. "Hey Billy, what's up?"

"Mom, mom, why didn't you answer? It's an emergency. You have to help Terrell. We were just walking up the walkway, and then the police were there, and then they shoved Terrell into the snow, and he was bleeding. Blood on the snow mom. It was so red. They took Terrell. They took Terrell, mom. You have to help."

"Billy. Slow down. I can't understand what you are saying. Did you say something about police? Are you okay?"

Celia listened patiently as Billy continued with the frantic account of his situation. When she finally understood enough of the basics, she cut him short and told him to wait where he was while she and Homer came to him. She'd have to learn the rest in person. Getting the straight story on the phone was nigh to impossible when he was in this state of mind.

"Perryville?" Homer asked. "Why on earth are they in Perryville?"

In the car, Celia tried to explain to Homer what Billy had said. The boys had been shoveling all afternoon, going from neighborhood to neighborhood throughout Sweetland, not realizing that at some point they stepped across the city limits into the small hamlet of Perryville out near Perry Pond. They walked up one long driveway and knocked on the door, prepared to shovel. They saw a woman peering at them from behind some curtains, but she didn't answer the door. They had gone back down the driveway to the next house.

"And at that house, they were invited to shovel?" Homer was still trying to connect the dots.

"Yes, that's right." Celia went on. "So they were shoveling, nearly finished, when a state police car pulled up beside them and—"

"Wait—you said State Police—why not Sweetland Police?"

"Perryville. Sweetland has no jurisdiction there. You know these small rural towns, they all rely on the Staties for law enforcement."

"Oh, that's right. Okay, continue." Homer said.

"Anyway, the State troopers jumped out of the car, pushed Billy aside, grabbed Terrell, and shoved him face down on the driveway. He got a bloody nose, and Billy was distraught at the blood all over the snow."

"I can imagine, Billy has always been a little squeamish. Never liked baiting or cleaning fish either."

"Well, I guess he tried to explain to the troopers that they were out shoveling driveways to make a little money, but suddenly Terrell was being hand-cuffed and shoved in the back seat of the car and whisked away. They said something about burglary charges and pointed to the house where they had seen the woman in the window. Billy is shaken up, of course. But I am sure it is all a big misunderstanding, so hopefully we can get it straightened out quickly. We'll pick up Billy and then head to the State Police barracks. We should call Hal and tell him to meet us there just in case Terrell didn't get a chance to call him yet."

Just as Celia concluded her story, they arrived at the house where Billy stood shivering at the bottom of the driveway. An older woman was standing with him, offering him a mug of something steaming hot.

"I'm Bernadette Green. This is my house. I offered to let your boy here come inside, but he wanted to wait out in the cold." She said, holding out her hand. After a quick handshake, she pointed to the house next door. "My neighbor is a bit paranoid. I guess when the boys walked up her driveway she thought she was being burglarized and called the police. So sorry these kids had to go through this when they were just being enterprising. I was happy to let them shovel my driveway. Twenty bucks well spent."

Celia thanked Mrs. Green and nudged Billy towards the car. As they drove to the State Police barracks some twenty miles away he repeatedly asked, "Why did they throw him down like that? And if they thought we were burglars, why didn't they take me too? I don't understand. It's not right."

"No, son, it's not right. But there are still some people, including some—but not all—police, who see a big strapping African American young man like Terrell and jump to the wrong conclusions. That's probably why they took him and not you. His grandfather Hal is meeting us there and I'm sure we'll get it straightened out. Try to calm down, okay?" Homer rested a hand on Billy's shoulder, adding, "I'm going to pray right now that wisdom, clarity, and justice will prevail. Relax, son."

~~

Neither wisdom nor justice prevailed on this day. Celia walked out to the car after two of the longest hours ever, feeling angry, cold, and frustrated. The State Police were intent on simply getting the paperwork done to transfer Terrell to the county lock-up pending a court appearance on Monday morning. They were not open to discussion. They didn't even let Hal see his grandson. They were all fuming as they huddled next to Hal's car and used Celia's phone to call their friend Randall Livingston, a policeman in Sweetland.

The connection was crackly on the remote rural road where the State Police barracks was located. No one could hear anything while Celia had the phone set to 'speaker,' so she clicked off the speaker function and held the phone to her ear. Several minutes later she ended the call with a steely look on her face.

"Randall is sympathetic, of course. Angry even. He's not working today but he's going to head over to the jail so he can be there when Terrell arrives. He will see what he can do, but given all the protocols and chains of command, he's not hopeful that he can do anything before court opens tomorrow morning. He's not even sure Terrell's adjudicatory hearing will be Monday or if they will wait until after the holidays."

Hal had been silent until now. "I kept my mouth shut the first time they arrested our boys for that fire last summer. Okay, so they did start the fire and they needed to be punished. I didn't like seeing them locked up, but I understood. But this? This is not right and I will not stand by silently. We have to do something. I can't just have a party and celebrate Kwanzaa with you all tomorrow and act like everything is normal when they are railroading my grandson." It was the longest speech Celia had ever heard Hal make.

A light bulb snapped on in Celia's mind. "That's it, Hal, you are a genius."

Hal looked startled and confused but waited for Celia to continue.

"Instead of a party for Kwanzaa, let's organize a vigil by the jail and courthouse, down on Sixth Street between Peach and Main. A peaceful protest. I think that will be a better way to honor the principles of Kwanzaa than just one more feast. What do you think?"

Homer's eyes lit up. "This is a perfect activity for the Sweetland Families for Justice. When we get home, I'll get the phone chain going. We'll bring a few posters, and hopefully Sophie and Bart will bring their drums. We'll focus on the principle of *Umoja: unity*. Unity in Sweetland behind the principle of justice for all."

Celia gave Homer a hug. "I love it when you get that fire in your eyes."

"I'm in." Hal said. "I'll make half the calls."

Billy looked back and forth at the adults around him, incredulous.

"No one knows what will happen tomorrow, but it is always right to stand up for what you believe, son." Homer said to Billy as the four got into their vehicles and drove away.

Chapter 4

December 29

Monday morning arrived in hues of gray. No more fresh snow had fallen, so the pristine beauty of the last few days had given way to a slushy, icy mess. The sky was the color of granite. It seemed fitting for the sense of foreboding settling into the pit of Celia's stomach.

Jan Symonds arrived at eight to take care of Sammy. His cold was a little better, but he was still not well enough to spend a day outside. *Thank you Lord for a neighbor like Jan, always ready to help out even on short notice.* Celia and Homer spent the next forty minutes on the phone, hoping to hear the good news that Terrell was being released and then they could cancel the hastily organized "Justice for Terrell and Umoja for Sweetland" vigil and peaceful protest scheduled to begin at ten o'clock.

Hal Jackson pulled into the driveway with Felix Batista. Within moments the entire Sweetland Families for Justice support group had arrived, several bringing family members and extra friends. Celia looked around at the organized chaos in her home. Dev and Jackie were working on the computer looking up some of their favorite Kwanzaa readings and related Bible verses to print on posters. Rocky and a few other youth who had arrived with their parents began transcribing the words onto large sheets of poster paper. Billy, who had been pacing all morning, made himself useful by serving coffee to the adults. CJ—oh dear—*where is CJ?* He could become easily overwhelmed in a situation like this and get himself into mischief. Celia made a mental note to find him as soon as possible before something got broken or someone got hurt.

At 9:45 Homer's cell phone rang. Everyone seemed to instantly know that this was 'the' call they had been waiting for with news from Randall Livingston. A hush fell across the room. Homer's expression said it all. No good news.

"Looks like the protest is happening. So let's load up the cars and head downtown. Remember, we are all going to park at Sweetland High near the football field and walk over to the corner of Sixth and Peach. Once we are lined up and have the posters in hand, Bart will start drumming and Felix will hand out the candles. No candles for small children—we don't want any fires. Most important thing is, no matter what happens, stay calm and peaceful. We want our voices to be heard and we don't want any unfortunate incidents to distract anyone from our messages, okay? Justice for Terrell and Umoja/Unity for Sweetland." Homer gave the marching orders calmly before sliding his arms into his winter jacket. "Don't forget gloves and hats. It may not seem too cold right now, but standing outside can chill the bones. Hope you all have your woolies on underneath. Join me in prayer for a moment before we head out."

As those gathered bowed their heads, Homer prayed, "Lord, you are the author of justice and you are the one who teaches us in Proverbs 31 to speak up for those who cannot speak for themselves and to ensure justice for all who are being crushed. You yourself remind us through your prophet Amos that you desire for justice to roll down like mighty waters, like a raging river, indeed, like a flood across the land. And you teach us that it is good and pleasant when your people come together in unity. Help us carry this message to the leaders of our community and bring about justice for Terrell Jackson today. Amen."

Celia, Homer, Dev, and CJ dispersed themselves into other people's cars so that Jackie, Billy and Rocky could take the family car. They would pick Vince up at the bus stop before coming to the vigil. "I'm proud of you, Mom, Dad, for planning this." Jackie said as they walked to the cars, "But I am kind of sad we aren't having our regular Kwanzaa party. Especially the sweet potato pie? You know? That's my favorite. I was really excited to share it with Vince."

"There might be some sweet potato pie before the end of the day." Homer said, winking at Jackie.

"What do you have up your sleeve, Homer Evers?" Celia asked.

Homer didn't reply. He just walked over to Felix Batista's car and hopped in the back seat.

~~

All seven cars that had been parked in the Evers's driveway pulled into the high school parking lot in a single file line. Adults and children scrambled out of the cars, zipping jackets, adjusting scarves and gloves, and handing out posters. Once assembled, the group walked across the street and up the block to stand just in front of the County Jail. Celia's mouth dropped open and her eyes began to tear as she saw the gathering of people already present. Word traveled fast in Sweetland, but she had no idea that so many of her fellow townspeople would give up part of their day to come out for this vigil. The first person she saw was Felix Batista's sister Juliet Venetti accompanied by Matt Evert. To their right, she noticed Arlene Smith's daughter Molly with her husband Max. *They must be in town for the holidays*, Celia thought. As she was scanning the crowd for more familiar faces, Kim Goodman, the new administrator of the Youth Acres Group Home, walked up and greeted Celia.

"Good morning Celia. Big day for Sweetland. Can you believe this crowd?"

"No, Kim, I'm stunned. Look, there's Dr. Finders. And mercy-me, Bob Lawrence. I never would have imagined him coming out for something like this. Who did you leave in charge up at Youth Acres?

"Roger is pulling a double shift. He worked last night, but he'll stay until I get back. A few of the girls are on home-visits with their families for the holiday week, so he can manage."

"Sounds good. Thanks for being here, I really appreciate the support."

"Wouldn't miss it. My parents and Carl are coming too. Thanks for taking the lead. You are braver than I am, Celia Evers."

"It's the youth themselves who inspire me. And speaking of youth, look who is here. The newly weds Rozene and Mike with the girls! Misty, Veronica, Shira, and Melanie—Jackie will be so pleased to see you all here."

Celia left the girls to catch up with Kim Goodman as she continued to scan the crowd. Felix handed out candles, and Bart started a slow, steady drumbeat. Children and teens eagerly began chanting, 'Justice for Terrell, Umoja for Sweetland' in time with the drums. She was relieved to see Billy and Dev walking her way, with Jackie and Vince behind them.

"So glad you made it, Vince. Hope the bus trip wasn't too rough."

"Thanks Mrs. Evers. It was worth it to be here. This is amazing. Do you think we can really make a difference?"

Before Celia could answer she was stunned to see Opal Barnett, the sweet old lady they met at the Labor Day picnic walking towards her, accompanied by a younger woman she didn't recognize.

"Celia Evers, I knew your family impressed me when we met on Labor Day, but today, my respect grows. This is Shondra. She works over at Breckenridge and she agreed to accompany me here so I wouldn't fall on my behind." Opal laughed. "Now let me answer that young man's question. Whenever you stand up for what you believe, you can make a difference. Never forget that. I want to tell you a story about that very thing if you care to listen to an old woman."

"Yes ma'am, I'd be happy to listen." Vince said.

"In 1963, I was thirty-one years old, minding my own business and not paying much mind to big events in the world. I had gone from my days as beauty pageant queen to wife and mother. That was my world. But we needed some extra money, so we took in a young man—about your age—as a boarder.

"That young man was full of idealism and big dreams about making the world a better place. In August, he took a bus trip all the way to Washington, DC to go hear some preacher by the name of Reverend Doctor Martin Luther King. I thought he had lost his mind. But I watched Mr. Cronkite on TV and I listened to every minute of it that I could. And I suddenly realized that my young boarder had much in common with one of my favorite people in the Bible. Queen Esther. She was just a young thing. But she stood up for her people even when it meant risking her own life. She made a difference.

"Dr. King made a difference. And today you can make a difference too. Never doubt that. Always speak up for truth. I'm old, but I had to come today. I wanted one last chance to make a difference. I didn't go on that bus trip in 1963, but by golly, I can be here today."

Opal's voice began to shake, and Shondra and Vince walked with her to a bench on the nearby sidewalk, urging her to sit down. She sat, but held her head high. Her eyes sparkled. She seemed far more confident than she had on Labor Day. Celia whispered a private prayer, *Lord, you brought her to this town when she thought she was old and washed up, and look how she is still making a difference in people's lives. Awesome.*

Two hours after the vigil began, Hal Jackson's phone rang. He was needed in court. Homer walked with his friend into the court building, and Celia held her breath. Moments later, Homer, Hal and Terrell emerged. Celia gasped at the sight of Terrell's bruised face and blackened eyes, but she felt immense gratitude at his release.

Terrell lifted his hands high into the air. "Umoja!" he shouted, "Umoja for Sweetland!"

At her side, CJ pulled on Celia's sleeve. "Look mom, everyone is happy. Just like that Bible verse. Everyone is together in unity. I think God is smiling."

With tears stinging her eyes, Celia pulled CJ close to her side murmuring, "Indeed, CJ, indeed; behold how good and pleasant it is!"

Chapter 5

January 1

"You're here; you have to work." Jackie said to Vince, pulling him into the kitchen, already crowded with Evers kids.

"Looks like you have enough help."

"On New Year's Day? There is never enough help. Preparing our fondue feast requires all hands on deck." Celia said, handing aprons to both Jackie and Vince. "You two can work at this counter over here. I have the cheese grating and vegetable chopping under control, so you can work on fruit for the chocolate fondue."

Soon Terrell and Hal arrived, and not long after that, Opal Barnett. What a treat to have these special guests to share in their family tradition. Celia took their coats and offered eggnog. With so many helpers, the preparations were finished efficiently and it was time to call everyone to the table.

"You start, Homer."

An audible groan came from all six of the Evers' children.

"Does dad have to make the same speech every year?" Rocky grumbled.

"Indeed, I do. And some day you will remember it fondly." Homer reached out and tousled Rocky's hair, eliciting a major eye-roll. Clearing his throat, Homer began, "We are so blessed to be able to gather with family and friends to start out the New Year. Fondue is a slow meal. Eat slowly, take your time. No rush. Our focus today is to remember everything we have to be thankful about from the year that just ended. Yes, we had hard times. We had challenges. We had fights, and sometimes we got hurt. But we have so much to be thankful for. So as each person takes their first forkful of fondue, share at least one thing you are thankful for with the rest of us. Who wants to start?"

"I will?" Jackie offered.

"Great, here's your fondue fork." Celia said, handing Jackie the fork with the green handle. "Remember your color."

"Duh, Mom. I know, right?" Jackie stabbed a chunk of Italian bread and a slice of Granny Smith apple with her fork and twirled it in the bubbling cheese fondue. "I'm thankful my friend Wendy got adopted this year. And I'm thankful I met Vince. And I'm thankful Dad got us Sweet Potato Pie from Deanie's Diner for Kwanzaa after the protest was over."

On that last note everyone started to laugh. Billy stepped up to be next.

"I think some of these things Mom and Dad make us do are stupid," he said. CJ gasped, and Sammy giggled. "But seriously guys, today, I am thankful for this family. We are the Evers, and we rock this town!"

Indeed we do. Celia thought to herself, *indeed we do. Thank you Lord. Umoja. Good and pleasant indeed.*

Nanna's Shortbread Cookies

Ingredients

2 cups of unsalted butter

2 tsp. pure vanilla extract

1 cup sugar

1 tsp. salt

4 cups flour

Directions:

Preheat oven to 350 degrees. Mix flour, salt and sugar. Cut butter into mixture in small (pea-size) pieces. Add vanilla. Mix with your hands until you can form a ball. Pat down on floured surface to ¼ inch thickness. Cut into shapes with your favorite cookie cutters and place on ungreased cookie sheet. Bake for 10-12 minutes. Edges and bottom should be lightly golden brown.

Optional: Dip half of finished cookie into melted dark or milk chocolate

Christmas Cranberry and Orange Scones

Ingredients

¾ cup butter (preferably unsalted)

1 cup dried cranberries

1 cup buttermilk

3 cups flour

¼ cup sugar

2 and a half tsp. baking power

½ tsp. baking soda

1 tsp. salt

1 TBSP orange zest, grated

Directions

    1. Preheat oven to 400 degrees.

    2. Prepare a cookie sheet by lining with parchment or waxed paper.

    3. Mix flour, sugar, baking powder, baking soda, salt, and orange zest.

    4. Cut small pea-size pieces of butter into flour mixture; work it with your fingertips until it resembles coarse meal.

    5. Stir in dried cranberries.

    6. Add buttermilk and mix in gently with a fork. Do not over-stir it.

    7. Sprinkle about 1/8th cup of flour to a wooden surface or pastry mat.

    8. Dump dough onto floured surface and begin to knead it gently, only about 4-5 times, just so it holds together.

    9. Press dough into a round shape, about ½ inch in thickness.

    10.   Cut the circle into up to 12 wedges (number may vary depending on the size scone you like.

    11.   Place wedges on prepared cookie sheet, leave at least ½ inch between each scone.

    12.   Bake 20-22 minutes, until edges and top of scones are golden brown

    13.   Serve with butter, cream cheese or clotted cream

To Make "No-Bake" Clotted Cream:

Start with 2 cups of heavy-whipping cream—*must not be ultra-pasteurized.* Line a strainer with 2 coffee filters or cheesecloth. Place over a bowl. Pour the heavy cream into the lined strainer. Refrigerate. Check it in two hours. The whey should have separated and drained to the bottom of the bowl. Pour off the whey, scrape the thickened cream back to the center of the filter and refrigerate again for 2 hours. Repeat. Do this every 2 hours until the clotted cream is the consistency of soft whipped butter.

Evers Family Homemade Eggnog

Note: This recipe uses raw eggs. It is important to purchase pasteurized eggs.

Ingredients

1 gallon whole milk

1 quart half and half

16 pasteurized eggs

2 and 2/3 cup sugar

4 TBSP cinnamon (more or less to taste)

4 tsp. nutmeg (more or less to taste)

8 TBSP pure vanilla extract

Optional 8 TBSP Rum flavoring

Vanilla Ice cream

Colored Sugar Sprinkles

Directions

1. Invite at least 3-4 children to help out. Make sure they all wash their hands and have aprons on.

2. Assign each child a task. One will measure milk, one will measure sugar, and so forth.

3. Make eggnog in small batches, placing 2 cups of milk, ½ cup of half and half, 2 eggs, 1/3 cup sugar, ½ TBSP cinnamon, ½ tsp. nutmeg and 1 TBSP vanilla into blender (and rum flavoring if using).

4. Allow children to blend on high speed until all ingredients are thoroughly blended.

5. Pour into punch bowl.

Optional: Add 3-4 small scoops of vanilla ice cream and colored sugar sprinkles to punch bowl before serving

Kwanzaa Sweet Potato Pie

Ingredients

1 and ½ cups cooked sweet potatoes

1/3 cup light brown sugar

¼ cup pure Vermont maple syrup

2 tsp. cinnamon

½ tsp. nutmeg

½ tsp. ginger

¼ tsp. ground cloves

½ tsp. salt

1 cup evaporated milk

2 eggs

1 TBSP butter

½ cup shredded coconut (you may use sweetened or unsweetened depending upon your preferences)

1 unbaked piecrust

Optional: Homemade whipped cream, extra coconut for garnish

Directions

Preheat oven to 400 degrees.

Mash sweet potatoes

Add sugar, maple syrup, cinnamon, nutmeg, ginger, cloves and salt and blend well

Melt butter

Lightly fork-beat eggs

Add butter, eggs and evaporated milk to sweet potato mixture, blend well.

Stir in coconut

Pour into piecrust

Bake 30-40 minutes (check after 30) until knife inserted into center comes out clean

Cool before serving

Optional: Serve with a dollop of homemade whipped and a sprinkling of coconut.

Happy New Year Salsa Fondue

<u>Ingredients</u>

12 ounces shredded sharp cheddar cheese (may use a combination of sharp and mild cheddar)

4 ounces shredded Monterey jack or Colby-jack cheese

1-2 TBSP flour

4 ounces of beer

2-4 ounces of fresh salsa

1 jalapeno, finely diced

<u>Items for Dipping</u>

Good French, Italian, Pumpernickel or other bakery breads, cut into 2-inch cubes

Granny Smith apples, cut into thick slices

Pretzels

Tortilla chips

Celery and Carrot Sticks

<u>Directions</u>

Mix cheeses in a large bowl, add flour and toss with your hands so that all cheese is lightly coated with flour.

In a double boiler, bring beer to a simmer.

Add floured cheese and stir constantly until cheese is melted.

Add salsa and diced jalapeno, stir until well blended.

Pour into fondue pot and serve immediately with dipping items.

4 SET FREE

Chapter 1

Wednesday, 9:30 AM

"In the final quarter of last year, we had particularly good numbers related to adoption of older youth; in fact it was the best quarter ever in that regard." Commissioner Walters beamed as she projected the latest child welfare data on the large screen in the conference room. Two dozen brightly frosted cupcakes from Deanie's Diner and Bakery sat on trays next to the projector as evidence that a celebration was in order. Celia smiled to herself, thinking of the roles that her own daughter Jackie and her good friend Rozene Gentry Carson played in helping the county Department of Social Services to achieve these numbers.

Not one to let good news linger, Commissioner Walters immediately clicked to the next slide, adding, "On the other hand, we've seen a sharp rise in very young children coming into foster care in our county, many of them exposed to the highly toxic environments of homes where meth is being produced. I've asked Josie McClellan from the county Substance Abuse Division to come to our meeting to help us understand this frightening trend." The face of Celia's phone lit up, indicating another missed phone call, just as Josie McClellan stood up to speak.

Hmmm, that's the third call I've missed from Jackie while in this meeting, Celia thought to herself. *I should probably send her a text to let her know I'm in meetings all morning.* In less time than it took for Celia's hand to discreetly slide the phone toward her lap, the screen lit up again. This time, it was a text from Jackie:

"MOM! U Nvr ans. Pls CMB asap"

Quietly, Celia set the phone or her lap and tapped out a reply:

"Can't talk. In mtgs. Will call back at noon. OK? Or Urgent?"

Within the space of two heartbeats, a reply appeared on the screen:

"Not urgent. Class at noon. Call at 2?"

After confirming that she would call Jackie at two o'clock, Celia turned her full attention to the staff meeting just in time to see horrific photos being posted of police wearing hazmat suits removing children from suspected meth homes. *"What a frightening experience for a young child. Lord, help us learn how to provide care for these children without adding to their trauma,"* Celia raised her hand to ask a question about funding for services.

By the time Josie McClellan turned the microphone back over to

Commissioner Walters, a few impatient colleagues had started passing the cupcakes around the room, noisily pulling the paper wrappers off and greedily scarfing up the tasty treats. When the tray reached Celia and her co-worker Barbara, it looked like a herd of kindergarteners had eaten, thrown, and played with the cupcakes until only a few random crumbs and smudges of frosting were left.

"I was worried about the temptation," Barbara said, frowning. "But now I see that my girlish figure will not be undone by an assault of morning sweets."

Celia poked her friend in the arm, snickering. "My husband works at Deanie's. Sometimes we get too many of these goodies. I am happy to pass this time around."

~~~

Celia worked through lunch, catching up on dozens of phone calls and emails. A few minutes before two, she stood and stretched her legs, then decided to walk outside to the little picnic table next to the parking lot. In the summer, this spot would be crowded with smokers, but on this chilly early-spring day, Celia was pretty sure it would be quiet enough for a private chat with Jackie.

"Mom?" Jackie answered in her lilting sing-song voice after less than one ring, "You called?"

"Two o'clock, right on the money," Celia laughed. Punctuality had never been her strong suit, but she worked hard at it. Structure, routine, and predictability in relationships were so important when caring for children whose early years were filled with trauma and loss.

"You never answer your phone, you know? But I can always count on you to call back. Thanks, Mom. I'm so excited, you know, I couldn't wait to tell you the good news!"

"Well, you've got me now, so spill it Jackster."

"Mom? You remember one of the most important reasons I wanted to go to Bethel-Morgan State College instead of going to the U like my other friends?"

"Bethel-Morgan has lots of selling points, but if I remember right, it was the track coach that you took a particular shine to."

"That's it, Mom. Right? But still even though she liked me and encouraged me last fall, I just wasn't sure. I didn't know what to think? You know? This is college, Mom, not high school, right?"

"Oh, you got that right. Your dad and I have the bills to prove it. So, I suspect there is something more to this conversation; I'm dying to hear it." Celia paused, squeezing her eyes shut, picturing her long, leggy daughter wearing a pair of pink running tights and bouncing on her toes, trying to find just the right words to share her news. A sudden burst of March wind played across the parking lot, sending cigarette butts, stray leaves, and a lone beer can in all directions.

"Jack? You still there?" Celia prodded her daughter to spit out the words she knew were hovering near the back of her tongue, waiting to be coaxed out.

"Yeah Mom, I'm still here. Soooooo the big news is–wait for it, wait for it–I made the track team! College track! Real stuff!"

"Ooooooohhhweeeeee, Jackie, I never doubted for a moment, but how exciting is this to hear the news! I'm so sorry I missed your calls earlier, this is big news, big, big news. We're so proud of you. When you come home for spring break over Easter, we'll have to figure out something fun to do to celebrate. What do you say?"

"Ah, well? That's the other thing, Mom. The students who make the team? We can't leave during spring break. We have practices and even our first meet coming up. Coach says we have to stay near campus, right? I'm sorry Mom, I hate to miss Easter, but this is really, really important."

"Duh, I should have thought of that myself, given the timing. No worries, Jack. It's all good. I'm pretty sure Easter will come to Bethel-Morgan State just as surely as it will come to Sweetland. You'll just have to check around and see if there are any Easter events you can participate in."

"I will, Mom. Thanks, you know? For understanding. Anyway, the dorms will be closed so the track team, we're all staying with families from town. I'll tell you more when I find out about it."

Celia shifted her position and checked the time. She and Jackie talked a few more minutes and then it was time to end the call and get back inside to work. What great news! Definitely better than a cupcake.

~~~

Celia eased her car into the crowded parking lot at Kelly's Food and Drug and strode inside, hoping to make this a quick stop. Grabbing a basket, she headed to the pasta aisle and nearly ran into her husband. "Homer? I didn't expect you to be here."

Homer maneuvered his heavily-laden shopping cart out of the stream of foot traffic. "You forgot? Today Hal, Felix, and I are buying the supplies for Saturday's spaghetti dinner. Randall is over at Discount Beverages picking up the water and soda, then we're all gathering at our house for a final meeting."

Celia smacked her palm to her forehead. "You're right. I did forget. Are you men cooking tonight, too?"

"No, just getting everything organized. But since we'll be commandeering the kitchen, I did order pizza for dinner." Homer said just as Hal came into their aisle with an equally full cart.

"Good evening, Celia."

"Hi Hal. Looks like you guys are planning to make enough spaghetti to feed the entire town of Sweetland."

"Yes, ma'am. If we want to raise enough money to get our boys all the way to Washington, D.C. we need to turn out all of Sweetland. New Beckton too, we hope, and maybe a few adventurous souls from Harrellsonville. Billy and Terrell and their friends Pete and Derrick are out putting up more flyers right now," Hal said while adding several boxes of spaghetti to his cart.

"I hope so, too," Celia said, adding, "I'm a little confused about all this shopping, though. I thought you said all the supplies were being donated."

"Kelly's Food and Drug donated a three hundred dollar gift card, but we still had to do the leg-work of buying the ingredients. Same thing at the beverage store," Homer said. "Oh a different note: now that you are here I have a favor to ask you. Looks like my van will be pretty filled with all this food so can you stop in at the after-school program and grab Sammy on your way home? Keep your eye out for Dev, too; he should be walking home from the library about now. And don't let me forget to talk to you about Rocky's field trip once we're both at home."

Celia pulled out her phone and checked the time. "Sure, I can do that, but looks like I better get going. See you at home. Oh—and I have some great news about Jackie," Celia teased as she turned and walked away from the two men.

Chapter 2

Saturday, 5:45 pm

Garlic, oregano, a hint of sage. Celia breathed deeply, taking it all in. The tantalizing aroma of simmering spaghetti sauce filled every corner of Fellowship Hall at the Presbyterian Church. In fifteen minutes, the doors would be opening. *Will people come?* She wondered. The Sweetland community often turned out to support good causes. More than a thousand people came to the concert hastily arranged to support the Williams family when their house burned down, and the fourth of July pancake breakfast to raise money for the summer youth programs always drew a crowd. *But will they turn out for a fundraiser to send boys who were in Juvie just a few months ago to a youth leadership conference in the nation's capitol? That remains to be seen.*

Celia surveyed the room, observing the final preparations. Rocky and her friend Kassidy McKenzie were taping paper streamers to the walls under the watchful eye of Jan Symonds. Sammy couldn't stand up to help, but he held the rolls of crepe paper on his lap in his wheelchair, enjoying the crinkling sounds they made every time he moved.

Across the room, a few teens from the community youth group worked with Dr. Gary Finders to organize the beverage table. Just inside the door, Dev sat at a small table with the money box, a roll of tickets, name tags, markers, and a receipt pad. Billy and Terrell manned a second table, covered with informational flyers about the Youth Justice Leadership Conference they hoped to be attending over spring break.

Homer was with most of the other members of the Sweetland Families for Justice Committee in the kitchen preparing vats of spaghetti, giant trays of garlic bread, and copious amounts of garden salad. All of her family members were accounted for except for CJ. *Oh CJ, what mischief are you finding this time?* Celia wondered as she walked towards the Sunday School rooms in search of her son.

Moments later, returning to Fellowship Hall with CJ at her heels, Celia gasped to see the line of people forming in the room. She caught a glimpse of Dr. Zack Michaelson and his wife Shellie, Kim Goodman with a few of the other staff from the group home and her own co-worker, Barbara Knight. Even better, she saw several people she didn't recognize at all. *Maybe Hal's prayers were answered and people are coming from Harrellsonville.* How gratifying to see such support!

Walking towards the kitchen to see if an extra hand was needed, Celia passed Rocky and Kassidy sitting on the edge of the stage, chatting in hushed tones. "Good job on the decorations, girls, it looks quite festive in here."

"Thanks, Mom. I hope you like the colors."

"I noticed they match the logo on the Youth Leadership Conference brochure. Pretty slick."

As if on cue, Rocky and Kassidy rolled their eyes in tandem, and then resumed their conversation. Celia heard the words "field trip" and remembered that the fifth and sixth graders had a big trip coming up next Friday, the last day before spring break. *That one will be fun to chaperone*, she thought to herself, imagining the possibilities presented by the potent combination of spring fever and moody middle-schoolers.

With Homer leaving the next morning for the D.C. trip, Celia had volunteered for that privilege.

"Mrs. Evers?" an unfamiliar voice called Celia's name before she reached the kitchen. Turning to her left, she saw a sturdy woman with her hand out-stretched standing next to two other women of similar age. "Bernadette Green," the woman said as Celia accepted the proffered handshake.

"Oh, Mrs. Green, I didn't recognize you without the snow," Celia said. "So glad you came tonight!"

"I wouldn't have missed it. Ever since I met your son and his friend shoveling my driveway, and all the unfortunate commotion that happened that day, I've tried to learn more about how we can do a better job helping young people stay on the right side of the law. These are my neighbors, Beverly Mills and Tomasina Corelli."

"Welcome," Celia said, shaking hands all around. "Please stop by the table over there and talk to Billy and Terrell. You can learn more about the leadership conference and what they hope to accomplish. I'm sure they will be especially happy to know you came out for the fundraiser." Before she could say more, Celia noticed Jan Symonds waving her hands to get her attention. "Excuse me, I have to check on my son." Celia said, walking away from the three women.

"What is it, Jan?"

"Sammy's been having a ball, with all the noise and activity here, but I think I should probably get him back to the house. He looks a little over-stimulated to me, and I'm remembering the last time he had that look it wasn't good."

Celia placed her hand on Sammy's forehead. No fever. But she, too, noticed that his pupils were more dilated than they should be and he had a bit of a rash around his neck. "Sammy, I think you've had enough excitement for one night. Miss Jan is going to take you home, now. Mom and Dad will be home later, okay buddy?" Turning to Jan, she added, "Jan you are a lifesaver. Thank you for coming out tonight and for being so attentive to Sammy."

"Happy to do it. You know Sammy is my favorite little champ," lowering her voice she added in a whisper, "Just don't let the other kids hear me say that."

They both chuckled as CJ bounced over in their direction. "CJ, Miss Jan is taking Sammy home now, would you like to go with them?" Celia asked.

"Why? You promised I could stay up late tonight. Plus, I told dad I would sweep the floor when everyone leaves and he's going to pay me!"

"Okay, you can stay. Just . . ." CJ scampered off before Celia could say another word.

~~~

The house was silent by the time Celia slid into bed next to

Homer. She reached for his hand, giving it a squeeze. "Great job tonight."

"It was a real team effort. I tell you, that Hal Jackson can cook. And it was really something to have the entire community youth group helping out. Gary Finders has done wonders with that group."

"He sure has," Celia said in agreement. "I don't know if you got much time out of the kitchen to see all the people that came. Opal Barnett was there, which didn't surprise me, but I was really shocked to see Bernadette Green and her neighbors. Do you remember her?"

"How could I forget? That episode with Billy and Terrell was the catalyst for deciding to get involved on the national scene with the juvenile justice reform work. I may not have noticed her, but she came back into the kitchen to say hello," Homer said, adding, "She wanted to introduce me to her neighbors. Did you know one of them is the same lady who called the police on Terrell?"

"No! For real? I didn't get to have much of a conversation with them because Jan was waving me down to check on Sammy. That's incredible, I wonder how she came to have such a change of heart?"

"I wondered that, too. It really made my night, and I thought Hal would pass out when he met her. God works in mysterious ways; that's all I can say."

"Indeed, He does. You must be bone tired."

"Yes, it was a long day. But I'm wired, too. Hope I can sleep tonight," Homer said, rolling to his side.

"Do you think you raised enough money?"

"Oh, I know we did. Dev already entered everything into his spreadsheet and gave me a report. Almost to the penny, we raised what we need to pay off the remaining expenses and for Billy and Terrell's needs. And also for Hal and I to go as chaperones. God supplied exactly what we prayed for," Homer said.

"I can't wait to see how God uses this trip. It could be a life-changer. But for now, I'm just so relieved that the people of Sweetland came out to show support. After all the uproar when the boys were first arrested, I wasn't sure what to expect."

"It wasn't just Sweetland. There were people there from Perryville and New Beckton, and even a few from Harrellsonville. Joe Turner from the Harrellsonville Daily News was there too. He came into the kitchen to interview some of us about why we started Sweetland Families for Justice. Maybe we'll get more support for getting those reforms at Juvie we've been pushing for."

Celia yawned. "Wow, that is exciting, Homer, but I don't think I can keep my eyes open for one more minute. You'll have to tell me more in the morning."

Chapter 3

Thursday, 5:00 am

Homer stepped into the living room balancing a basket of
laundry on his hip. He looked surprised to see Celia sitting next to the
fireplace, coffee in hand. "You're up early."

"So much going on in the next few days. Hard to sleep," Celia
replied.

"I'm about to get another cup of coffee; do you need a refill?"

"No, I'm all set." Celia watched Homer set the laundry down
and walk toward the kitchen. Absent-mindedly, she began folding
laundry, thinking about everything she had to do in the next two days.
Today, she had a court hearing on the Judson case and a supervisors'
staff meeting at work. She also had to make sure the little Roland girl
had a placement to go to as soon as she was released from the hospital.
She'd need a foster parent who wouldn't be squeamish about caring for
those burns. Everything had to be finalized today so she could take
tomorrow off to go with Rocky's class on the field trip to the Science
Museum in Harrellsonville. *Why on earth did I sign up for that?*

"I should take a picture," Homer said as he came back into the
room.

"Of what?" Celia looked around to see what could possibly be photoworthy at this time of morning.

"You. Folding laundry. I think it may have happened before. Once. Back in 1986."

"Very funny," Celia replied, throwing the sweatpants she was folding at her husband, causing a splash of coffee to slosh out of his mug.

"You know it's true. And now, look, I'll have to wash these sweats again. Lot of help you are."

"Oh hush. You know, even though you pick on me endlessly…."

"Ummmm, endlessly."

"Yes, endlessly," Celia smiled. "Even though you pick on me, I'm going to miss you next week. Hard to believe you and Billy will be gone for an entire week."

"I know. I don't think we've had that much one-on-one time ever. After all the work getting ready for it, I can't believe this trip is finally almost here. I just wish we didn't have to be away over Easter, though."

"Yes, with you and Billy in D.C. and Jackie at college, it will be different here, that's for sure. It's all good, but still it makes me a little blue."

"Speaking of Jackie, has she called again?"

"Last night, actually," Celia said. "She told me about the family she will stay with while the dorms are closed. They have two grown children and they were going to be alone for Easter, so they volunteered to take a couple of kids from the college. Jackie and another girl from the track team will stay with them."

"That's good, is she nervous about her first meet tomorrow?"

"Hard to read—you know how she is with her emotions. But she was excited to tell me that some of her friends from Sweetland are going to go to the meet on their way home from the U for spring break. Veronica and Shira and Melanie—the girls Rozene adopted."

"A regular reunion. Sounds great. Do those girls have their own car now?"

"Yes, Rozene got them an old beater to get back and forth from college. Also, apparently Veronica has a new boyfriend, and he's doing the driving."

"That's an interesting development. Hope this young man meets Rozene's approval. She can be a tough cookie sometimes."

"True," Celia said. "But ever since she and Pastor Mike got married, she has softened."

"Mike's a good man. But really, I think it was bringing Misty into her life and then the other girls, that's what softened her heart."

"You're right about that. And Misty has blossomed as a result. They all have, actually." The sound of a flushing toilet upstairs indicated that the official morning routine in the Evers' household was about to begin. Celia snatched the last t-shirt out of the laundry basket to fold. "Guess it's time to get moving. Busy day ahead. Oh, and there is a planning meeting for the community Sunrise Service tonight. I'll go over there directly after work, so don't hold dinner for me."

~~~

Returning from court, Celia had just forty minutes to review the list of foster homes with open beds and decide which family to call first about the Roland girl before she had to leave for the planning meeting at Community Church. She retrieved a granola bar from her purse, not sure when or if she'd get any dinner. The light on her desk phone began to flash. Annoyed at the interruption, she snatched up the receiver.

"Celia, I'm sorry to bother you, but it's someone from the after-school program. It's about Sammy and they said it's urgent," the DSS administrative assistant, Angie, informed Celia before transferring the call.

Seconds later, Celia stopped by Barbara's desk, asking her to please locate a placement for the Roland girl and then rushed out the door. Sammy hadn't had seizures in at least three years. Why now, with so much else going on? How was she going to juggle a child in the hospital, an out-of-town field trip and all the Easter activities alone with Homer and Billy in D.C.?

"I hope everything will be okay with your son, Celia." Angie called after her as she reached the elevator.

That comment stopped Celia in her tracks. *Lord forgive me for my self-centered thoughts. This isn't about me and everything I have to do. This is about Sammy. Please watch over my little boy, Lord, help him not to be scared until I get there.*

~~~

Celia stood at the bedside of her sweet son, tears rimming her eyes as she listened to the doctor. This was the worst set of seizures Sammy had ever had and now he was totally limp and unresponsive.

"I'm afraid we are not best equipped to treat him here, Mrs. Evers. He will be better served at Children's Hospital in Harrellsonville. I've arranged for a transfer, I just need you to sign these papers."

Celia scribbled her name, asking, "May I ride in the ambulance with him? I don't want him to be terrified when he wakes up."

"Yes, that's fine. Follow me, we're ready to go now."

Stopping briefly at the nurse's desk, Celia asked Anne Goodman to please tell Homer what had happened, and then she trotted off to catch up to the stretcher rolling Sammy toward the elevators.

In the ambulance, Celia was not allowed to use her cell phone. She'd been unable to reach Homer earlier, so she'd left a voice mail message letting him know that Sammy was at Sweetland Hospital. Now they were careening off to Harrellsonville and she had no way to fill him in.

~~~

Sammy was settled snuggly in bed, with tubes and wires protruding in all directions. The unmistakable blend of hospital smells was overwhelming. Children's Hospital's cheerful décor accented with stuffed animals and primary colors did little to calm her anxious heart. It had been nearly two hours and still no word from Homer. Where was he?

Just then, the door to Sammy's room swung open. "I got here as quickly as I could." Homer rushed to the bedside and tousled Sammy's hair. "Thank God he's alive."

"Alive? It's serious Homer, but he's going to be fine; why would you say that?"

"When I got your message, I made arrangements for the kids at home and then went to Sweetland Hospital," Homer said. "I must have looked a little lost, because a young orderly came up to me, asking if I needed help."

"The new kid? That's Nathan, Arlene Smith's nephew."

"Could be, I didn't get his name. I told him I was looking for Sammy Evers and he said, 'Oh, I'm sorry sir, Sammy is no longer with us.'"

"What?" Celia gasped.

"I almost fell on the floor. I really thought Sammy had died. I couldn't imagine…I just, I, I was speechless."

"Oh Homer, what a heartless thing for that young man to say," Celia stood and hugged Homer tightly.

"He didn't mean any harm. As soon as he saw the look on my face, he started talking very fast. That's when I realized he was simply trying to tell me Sammy had been transferred here."

"Someday we'll laugh about that one."

"Yeah, maybe."

A nurse entered the room and approached Sammy's bed to get his vitals. Homer removed his coat and paced back and forth in the tiny space. He asked the nurse a few questions as she went about her work efficiently. As soon as she left the room, he cleared his voice to speak. "I'm not sure what to do about this D.C. trip. Billy is really looking forward to it and the whole community contributed funds to make it possible."

"Stop, Homer. Everything will be fine. You and Billy need to go on the trip. Tomorrow you stay here with Sammy while I go on the field trip with Rocky's class and then I will come back here. I'll talk to Jan and we'll figure out coverage for everything while you are gone."

"Jan's at the house now," Homer said.

"That's good. Don't worry. Aren't you the one always telling me to have faith in these kind of circumstances?" Celia clasped Homer's hand. "Sammy is stable and getting good care here. Frankly, I'm more worried about coping with that field trip tomorrow." Celia tried lightening the mood.

"What could possibly go wrong on a field trip with ninety-five middle-schoolers?" Homer asked. Sammy stirred. "Even Sammy knows that's a ridiculous concern."

Chapter 4

Friday, 11:15 AM

So far, so good. Celia thought to herself as she surveyed the group of nine girls she'd been assigned to watch at the Science Museum. *Rocky, Kassidy, Madison, Joanie, Flynn, April, Kylie, Jill and . . .* "Evelyn, have you seen Mo'nee?" Celia asked the other chaperone.

Evelyn Cole nodded and pointed to the restroom. It looked like she was talking, but Celia couldn't hear a word. Between the excited children and the metal clanging of the contraption in the hall below—demonstrating electro-magnetism or something of the sort—the noise in this part of the museum was deafening. She edged a little closer so she could hear.

"She needed the bathroom. I told her we'd all wait right here before meeting the rest of the class for lunch," Evelyn repeated. "It's going better than I thought it would. I have to confess, I was a little nervous. This is the first time I've been a chaperone for an out-of-town field trip."

"I agree," Celia said. "I had all kinds of worries. Homer usually handles the daytime school events while I work. I didn't really know what to expect, but it's actually been fun, a nice break from my usual routine. I have to tell you, it's wonderful to see how well Joanie is doing in your care."

"Thank you. Ron and I just can't imagine our life without James and Joanie. It's as if they've been part of our family forever."

Celia opened her mouth to reply, but stopped short when two security guards rushed past her and charged into the girls' restroom. A booming alarm bell sounded, and a red light began flashing in the hallway. Joanie ran up to Evelyn Cole, clutching her hand. The other girls stopped their conversations and gaped. *Mo'nee!* Celia suddenly remembered that one of their charges was inside that rest room. She hurried toward the door.

As soon as Celia got inside the rest room, the noises from the hallway faded into the background and all she could hear was an eerie keening sound coming from the back corner of the room. One of the security guards was barking into a walkie-talkie and grasping her baton.

"What's happening?" Celia asked, rounding the corner in time to see Mo'nee standing on the windowsill, wailing.

"You'll have to get out of here, Miss," the older guard said to Celia, grasping her elbow and strongly urging her back toward the door.

"No, I need to stay. That little girl is one of my charges. I'm a chaperone for this field trip. Please, tell me what's going on." Celia shook herself loose from the grip of the guard and crept quietly closer to Mo'nee.

"We'll get someone to talk to you after the scene is stabilized." The second guard said, stepping in between Celia and the still-screaming child.

"I'm sorry. I'm not leaving," Celia said firmly. "Besides being a chaperone, I'm a social worker with the Department of Social Services, and this is a child in our custody." She flashed her ID quickly to the guards and then turned her full attention to Mo'nee. "Sweetheart, I can see that you don't feel safe here, but I'm going to stay with you, and I promise everything will be okay."

"No, no, no, no," Mo'nee screeched. "Everybody needs to go away. Go away, go away!"

"I'm going to stay right here with you. I'm not going anywhere until you feel safe again, Mo'nee. Can you breathe with me?" Celia started taking slow, deep breaths, urging the child to mimic her rhythm. Celia looked around, taking in the scene. Nothing seemed out of place except for a few crumpled paper towels on the floor. In the opposite corner, a mop and bucket stood unattended. The room was filled with the odor of pine-scented cleaning solution. The sound of water dripping from one of the faucets behind her became evident as Mo'nee's sobs abated. Not taking her eyes off Mo'nee, she again asked the guards, "What happened?"

"The cleaning lady called. She said there was a crazy girl in the restroom. Screaming like a banshee. Cleaning lady felt threatened. She thinks the girl is on drugs. We have to assess the situation and wait for the police to arrive."

"Police?" Celia was dumbfounded. This was a scared little girl.

"We don't know what's wrong with this kid. She might be a safety risk to others."

"What's wrong with her?" Celia asked, "Maybe we need to turn that question around and ask whatever might have happened to her to cause her to be so terrified in this restroom?" Mo'nee had stopped wailing, but continued to clutch the edges of the windowsill as if hanging on for dear life. "I can tell you one thing, this child is not a threat to anyone, but if you bring the police in here she will be further traumatized. Please just let me have some time with her. Alone."

"Can't do that, ma'am. We have a policy," the younger guard said.

"We'll stand right outside the door," The second guard interrupted, opening the door and stepping out. The first guard hesitated, then followed, propping the door open a few inches with a wooden doorstop.

Talking in quiet, soothing tones, Celia spent several minutes trying to calm Mo'nee. Finally getting her off the windowsill, she gently placed an arm over her shoulder and waited until the child's breathing became regular. "Do you want to talk?"

The girl shook her head.

"Okay. Are you hurt anywhere?"

Another shake of the head.

"Hungry?"

No response.

"I think the other girls are waiting for us. Let's go have some lunch. I promise I'll sit with you, okay?" Celia gently guided the somber child into the hallway. Out of the corner of her eye, she noticed her daughter Rocky's rigid posture.

~~~

Feeling as though her head would explode, Celia rummaged around in her desk drawer for some Advil. Thankfully, the rest of the field trip was uneventful and all the students were safely reunited with their parents. Celia had come into her office to write up the incident report and call Mo'nee's foster parents before heading back to stay with Sammy at the hospital in Harrellsonville. She stole a glance across the room, observing Rocky sitting by the window, reading.

"Homer? Just checking in. How's Sammy doing?" Celia called the hospital first to give Homer a head's up that she would arrive later than planned. After getting an update on Sammy's condition, she continued, "There was an incident on the field trip, and I had to stop by the office for a few minutes. I have Rocky with me; she wants to see Sammy and then she'll ride home with you…. No, no, the incident didn't involve Rocky directly, although she is shaken. I'll fill you in more in person. Hopefully I'll be there in an hour or so; I know you still have things to do to get ready to leave in the morning."

Celia ended the call and walked across the room, coming to a stop next to Rocky. Squatting down to face her daughter at eye level she looked her up and down for any signs of stress. Thankfully, Rocky looked fine. *Looks can be deceiving, I know, I know. We'll have time to talk in the car.* "Rocky, I have to make a couple of phone calls and write up a short report. Then we can leave to go to the hospital. Do you need some water or anything while you're waiting?"

Rocky shook her head without looking up from her book. Overhead, the fluorescent lights hummed. Down the hall the swishing of a mop was the only other sound in the building.

Celia walked back to her desk and punched in the numbers for Dinah Collins, Mo'nee's foster mother. "Hello, Mrs. Collins? This is Celia Evers at DSS. I wanted to check in with you on Mo'nee now that she has been home for a little while. How is she doing?"

Celia held the phone in her right hand, closed her eyes and rubbed her temples with her left hand, listening to the concerned tone of the voice on the other end of the line. *Please Lord, don't let her ask me to remove Mo'nee from her home. This little girl needs stability more than ever right now.*

"Ms. Evers? I really don't want Mo'nee to have to move. But I have the other children to worry about. This is the fourth time she has done something like this right out of the blue. She flies into these violent rages for no apparent reason. So far no one has been hurt, but my husband and me, we're worried. We're not sure what to do. We just don't know what's wrong with this one."

There was that question again, "What is wrong with this child?" Celia had heard that too many times today. She wanted to take out a full-page ad in the newspaper saying, "*Whenever you are wondering what is wrong with a child, ask what may have happened to the child instead. You could be the first link in the chain of healing.*"

Celia turned to her keyboard and tapped a few notes into her computer, composing her thoughts. "I appreciate your honesty, Mrs. Collins. I know it's so hard to watch a child struggle and not be able to make sense of it. From my observations today, I would guess that she was having some sort of trauma reaction. Something in that restroom may have triggered her. Tell me, have any of these incidents occurred at your home or have they all been somewhere else?"

Several minutes later, reassured that Mo'nee was safe for the evening and that Mrs. Collins was prepared to hang in there with the child, Celia hung up the phone and called to Rocky to get her coat and backpack.

~~~

After riding in silence all the way up Mt. Laurel Street and for several miles across State Highway 8, Rocky, still looking away from her mother and staring out the passenger-side window, spoke up. "Mom, I know I'm not supposed to listen to your phone calls, but I heard you say something about a trigger to Mo'nee's foster mother. Was there a gun in that restroom?"

Celia paused for a moment, trying to gauge how much to say to her pre-teen daughter. Drawing a breath, and remembering her honesty-is-best policy, Celia plunged into the truth. "No, Rocky, no gun. I'm sorry if hearing that alarmed you. I was speaking of a different kind of trigger. A trauma trigger. Sometimes when someone has experienced something very scary or painful in their past, something new can happen in the present that makes them feel as though they are reliving the bad thing again. That new thing, that's what is called a trauma trigger. I'm not completely sure, but I suspect that is what happened to Mo'nee today."

"Oh." Rocky remained silent.

The road curved to the left and then quickly to the right. A stand of trees appeared and then the Harrellsonville city skyline came into view. A minute passed and then two. Still, the girl beside her said nothing. Celia felt her palms become damp against the steering wheel. Had she said too much?

"Remember when you first adopted me and CJ?" Rocky turned away from the window, facing her mother.

Celia kept her eyes on the road. "I sure do."

"CJ was so scared of dogs. It seemed like he turned into a statue and couldn't move whenever a dog was around. Do you remember that?"

"Yes, Rocky, I do remember that." Celia turned on her left directional. They were just a few blocks from Children's Hospital.

"And water. He never liked water, especially not swimming over at Perry Pond on those really hot days."

"Yes. That's right. He'd always run off to climb trees while everyone else was swimming. He was like a little monkey in those trees."

"Mom, I think dogs and the pond, I think those were trauma triggers for CJ. I remember a long time ago, before we met you and dad, we had a dog. The dog died in the pond. No. He drownded. My first dad was yelling at our mom saying they didn't have enough food for us kids, how could she feed a dog, too? CJ was crying that day."

Celia pulled a parking ticket from the machine at the hospital garage and waited for the arm to rise so they could enter the lot. "I never knew that story, Rocky. Thank you for sharing it with me." She maneuvered the car into a parking spot, shifted into park and reached over to give her daughter a hug.

"He's better now. Do you think Mo'nee will be better one day, too?"

"I hope so, Rocky. I really hope so."

Chapter 5

Saturday, 5:30 am

Celia stirred, disoriented for a moment as the door to the hospital room creaked open. Expecting to see a nurse, she was shocked to see Randall Livingston's lanky frame fill the doorway. Alarmed to see the police officer in this setting, Celia sat up abruptly. She glanced quickly at the sleeping form of Sammy on the bed beside her. Except for the raspy breathing he seemed fine.

Officer Livingston tipped his hat, smiling. "Good morning, Celia."

"Good morning, Randall. Who? What?" She couldn't quite get her words together.

"Oh there's no problem at all," he said, evidently reading the fear and confusion etched on her face. "A few of us from the Sweetland Families for Justice group met at your house last night to make sure Hal and Homer and the boys were all set for the big trip today. We got to talking and we thought you might like to see them off this morning. I don't work today, so I said I'm come over here and sit with Sammy so you can go home for a few hours."

This was totally unexpected. When Celia sent Homer and Rocky home last night she hadn't expected to see him again for a week. "Randall, I don't know what to say," she said.

"No need to say anything, but you best get a move on if you want to make it back to Sweetland before they have to catch the bus out of town." Randall removed a folded sheet of paper from his back pocket. "Oh, and another thing, we made some phone calls last night. We talked to your pastor and some folks from your church and Community Church. We know you have to work next week, so we lined up coverage for you while Homer is gone. This here is the schedule." He thrust the paper towards Celia.

Celia unfolded the sheet and stared. It seemed as though the whole town had stepped up to help her family. People had signed up for shifts at the hospital with Sammy, at home with her other kids and even to bring meals each day straight through until Friday. Good Friday. Amazing.

A nurse poked her head into the room. "Is our boy still asleep?" she queried.

"He is."

"I'll come back to wash him up and get vitals in a few minutes. Do you need anything, Mrs. Evers?"

"No, I'm fine. But I'm about to leave for a few hours. I'd like to introduce you to our friend, Randall Livingston. He'll stay with Sammy until I get back. And I'll have my cell phone if you need me."

Smiling flirtatiously at Randall, the nurse turned and left the room. Celia snatched her jacket from the back of the chair and tiptoed to the door, not wanting to wake Sammy.

~~~

Stepping out of her car, Celia immediately noticed CJ standing just inside the kitchen door, bouncing from one foot to the other. "What are you doing up so early, champ?" She asked as she walked inside.

"There was too much noise around here. Who can sleep?" Behind him, Homer and Hal Jackson burst into laughter.

"You woke me up, CJ. I wasn't making any noise," Homer said.

Celia glanced around the room. Four suitcases and sleeping bags were lined up next to the door. Hal and Homer each held a steaming mug of coffee in their hands while Billy and Terrell sat slumped in their chairs, looking barely awake. Slipping off her jacket, Celia walked to the counter and poured herself a cup of coffee and then joined the men at the table. "Looks like the troops are ready for a long trip."

Celia described Sammy's night to Homer and then asked for an update from the home front.

After filling Celia in on Dev, Rocky and CJ's plans for the day and reviewing the coverage schedule that Randall Cunningham had given her, Homer paused, then added, "Oh, I don't want to forget—good news. Jackie called last night. She placed second in the hundred meters and third in the four-by-four relay. Not half bad for her first meet as a college girl."

"That is good news. Did her Sweetland girlfriends make it in time to see her run?"

"They did. She was very happy about that. If you want to talk to her, I'd wait till sometime after noon. I suspect she'll be sleeping all morning."

"Sleeping. That's what I want to do. Can we get to the bus so I can go back to sleep?" Billy grunted.

Homer looked at the clock and nodded. "Load 'em up and move 'em out," he said to Hal and Celia. Lingering at the door after the others headed to the car, Homer circled his arms around Celia's waist. "I'm torn. I'm really looking forward to this week with Billy, but I hate leaving you here alone with Sammy in the hospital, and missing Easter with the family. I especially hate missing the community Cross Walk on Friday—that's one of my favorite events every year."

Celia returned the hug and added a kiss. Breaking away, she patted Homer lightly on the backside, saying, "Scoot. After all this planning we can't have you missing the bus. Everything will be fine here. Call or text when you get a chance. Now go."

~~~

Thursday, 3:00 pm

Celia sat with Dinah Collins sipping a soothing cup of chamomile tea. The living room had a cozy-but-lived-in feeling. A six-month-old baby slept contentedly in the port-a-crib behind the couch. Rows of school photos lined the walls. A stack of mail competed with coloring books, crayons and puzzle pieces for space on the table next to the TV.

"I think I made a discovery," Dinah said, "about Mo'nee and that idea of trauma triggers you told me about."

"A discovery? That sounds intriguing. Fill me in." Celia lifted her tablet out of her purse and powered it on so she could take notes.

"I should really give credit to my husband Russ," she continued. "After we talked the other night, I was trying to explain everything you told me. Russ thinks you were talking about PTSD. He knows about that because his uncle served in Vietnam. He was never the same again after he came home. But we didn't think children could get PTSD. Can they?"

Celia reached into her purse again and retrieved a book, *Wounded Children, Healing Homes* by Jayne Schooler. Sliding the book across the table, she said, "I'm glad you mentioned that. This is what I wanted to talk to you about today. I've been thinking more and more about what happened at the museum. I've re-read Mo'nee's file, and while I can't find anything specific, I am convinced that she was reacting to something from her history that day. I know you don't have a lot of time to read while caring for all these children, but I think you will find this book helpful."

Dinah picked up the book, thumbed through it and set it back down on the table. She stood to check on the sleeping baby and came back to her seat. "Russ will be pleased as punch to know that he was on the right track. He said his uncle had particularly bad reactions to certain smells. Like smoke. And, well, urine."

Celia listened, thinking about the chain of events at the museum last week. *Urine? I wonder....*

As if reading her mind, Dinah said, "When he mentioned urine, I thought maybe that was the trigger for Mo'nee since, you know, the episode happened in the rest room. But then I started thinking about the other times she had those outbursts. They weren't in restrooms at all."

Across the room, the baby stirred, gurgled, rolled over and then drifted back to sleep. A fat tabby cat meandered into the room and plopped heavily next to the couch.

Dinah went on, "So I made some notes. And that's when I think I made a discovery. I don't know what that bathroom at the museum smelled like, but if they use some kind of pine-scented cleaning liquid, that might be it. All the other incidents took place at my sister's house. My sister loves the scent of pine and she always has pine air fresheners and pine candles around the house. I don't know if that means anything, but I just thought I would mention it."

Celia instantly remembered the odor of the pine-scented cleaning liquid in the science museum restroom. She entered a few notes on her tablet and nodded. "You could be on to something, Mrs. Collins. There was, indeed, a pine scent in that bathroom. We can't jump to conclusions. We may never learn what her actual triggers are, but it's good to be observant. In the meantime, the most important thing for you and Russ is to help Mo'nee believe she's safe, and to help her learn some self-calming techniques she can use when she begins to feel unsafe. When I got her to breathe slowly with me last week that seemed to help, so I'd encourage you to help her develop breathing techniques. One that we use in our own family is blowing bubbles."

"Bubbles?"

"That's right," Celia said, pulling a small bottle of bubbles out of her purse. "We keep these bottles all over the house. Bubble-blowing is calming, soothing and helps children develop controlled breathing."

Dinah Collins peered over the edge of the table and stared at Celia's purse. "Do you have any more surprises in that bag?" she asked, reaching for the bottle of bubbles.

~~~

Celia pulled into the parking lot at Kelly's Food and Drug. She had just enough time to pick up the few items she needed, drop them off at home, and drive to Children's Hospital to relieve Kim Goodman, who was sitting with Sammy. She was mentally reviewing her shopping list when her phone began to vibrate on the seat beside her. A quick glance revealed that the incoming call was from the hospital. Steeling herself for bad news, Celia picked up the phone and tapped the "answer" icon.

"Really? Today? Oh that is wonderful news…. Yes, I can be there in thirty minutes. Thank you." *Thank You, Lord!* Celia breathed a quick prayer as she re-started the car. Sammy was ready to come home. The groceries could wait.

Chapter 6

Saturday

Celia stood next to Dr. Gary Finders, watching the youth group students join with a handful of adults to assemble the bleachers for the Sunrise Service to be held early the next morning. Homer and Billy would be helping if they were here. She missed them terribly at this moment. Tears started to push their way into her eyes, but seeing Will Smith and Carlie Parsons arriving together, made her smile. *Hmmmm, another Easter miracle? First Sammy, now Will and Carlie? What else is up your sleeve, Lord?*

"Mrs. Evers, what do you think?"

Celia turned her head to see Jackie's friends Veronica and Melanie draping purple and white fabric around the rails of the gazebo. Smiling, she gave them two thumbs up and then turned back to Dr. Finders. "Tim, it doesn't look like there's much left to do. I think I'm going to head home—I wanted to help, but I didn't want to leave Sammy for too long."

"I understand, Celia. Everything is under control here. Dev and Rocky can stay if they want; I'd be happy to drop them off at home when we finish here. Where is CJ? I haven't seen that little scamp all day."

"Thanks, Gary. I'm sure Dev and Rocky would be happy to stay. Oh, and CJ--he's spending the afternoon with the Coles. He and James have been overdue for a play date, so today worked out great. They are really a little young—and maybe overly energetic— to be helpful here."

Driving home, Celia couldn't shake the blue feeling that had settled around her shoulders while at City Park. Easter just wasn't going to be the same without Homer, Billy, or Jackie at home. And Sammy wasn't strong enough to be outside in the morning air, so she'd have to miss the Sunrise service, too. She didn't even really have the energy to make Easter baskets for the kids. They were getting older; maybe she could skip it this year. *CJ is still a little boy, and Sammy, too. Stop being lazy.*

~~~

With the last of the dishes finished and Sammy sleeping soundly, Celia pulled a book off the shelf and sat in her favorite chair. CJ and Rocky were watching TV, but Dev wasn't in sight. *Probably on his computer.* Finding the place she'd left off, Celia began to read. Her eyes were getting heavy; it had been such a long week.

"Mom. Mom, are you sleeping?" Dev stood next to Celia's chair calling her over and over.

"No, just resting my eyes," Celia said.

"Ha, that's dad's line," Dev replied.

"So it is. But he's not here, so I think I'm entitled to use it. So, now that you've aroused me from my non-sleeping state, what can I do for you?"

"Nothing."

"Okay, so….."

"I want to do something for you," Dev said.

This was getting interesting. Celia looked around the room. Rocky and CJ were no longer watching TV. "Where are Rocky and CJ?"

"It's after ten o'clock, Mom. I told them to go to bed."

Celia bolted in her chair. Had two hours really passed since she sat down?

"I know how much you love that Sunrise Service on Easter," Dev said. "And CJ and Rocky are always up early. So I was thinking, I could stay home with Sammy so you guys could go."

"Oh Dev, I don't know. I should probably stay home with Sammy."

"Mom. Everyone else has been helping out all week, so, I thought I could do my share. I'll read the Easter story to him or something, I promise."

Celia took note of the earnest look on Dev's face. How could she say no?

~~~

Easter Sunday, dawn

The crowd settled back onto their bleacher seats after singing the last lines of "Up from the Grave." After a moment of silence, four members of the ecumenical liturgical dance team stood with their backs to the audience. Pastor Mike stood at the microphone, turning pages in his Bible.

"A reading from Luke, chapter four, beginning on verse sixteen," he began, continuing:

> *And He came to Nazareth, where He had been brought up; and as was His custom, He entered the synagogue on the Sabbath, and stood up to read. And the book of the prophet Isaiah was handed to Him. And He opened the book and found the place where it was written,*
>
> *"The Spirit of the Lord is upon Me,*
>
> *Because He anointed Me to preach the gospel to the poor.*

The first dancer turned, faced the audience and gracefully moved across the lawn.

> *He has sent Me to proclaim release to the captives,*

The second dancer turned and faced the audience, revealing chains binding her wrists and ankles. She burst into dance, breaking the chains and leaping joyfully across the lawn.

And recovery of sight to the blind,

The third dancer turned and faced the audience, revealing heavy blindfolds across his eyes. He tore them loose and twirled magically, stopping next to the first two.

To set free those who are oppressed,

The fourth dancer turned and dropped heavily to the ground. After a silent moment, she leapt into the air and joined hands with the other three dancers. Together, they encircled the Pastor while he read the final portion of the passage. The first glimmers of sunlight washed the park in hues of gold and pink.

To proclaim the favorable year of the Lord."

And He closed the book, gave it back to the attendant and sat down; and the eyes of all in the synagogue were fixed on Him.

A short time later the powerful service concluded with the final hymn. Celia, CJ and Rocky descended from their seats on the bleachers and began walking to their car.

"Mom? I was thinking."

"Yes, Rocky?"

"I liked that dance. And the Bible words that went with it."

"I did too. Very moving."

"Me too. It was cool, especially when that one dancer busted out of the chains," CJ added.

"Anyway, Mom. I was so mad this morning. I was mad at God," Rocky said.

"Mad at God?" Celia didn't understand.

"I was mad about Easter. It didn't seem fair. You know. Jackie's not home, and Dad and Billy. And then Sammy was too sick to come, so Dev and him had to stay home. I mean what kind of Easter was it going to be with just you and me and CJ. No offense."

"Hmmm, yes, I see. I'm not offended, it's okay. I was feeling a little sad and missing all of them, too."

"But then they did that dance, and I started thinking. If Easter is about helping people who are blind, like Sammy, or in chains like kids at Juvie, or you know, oppressed like Mo'nee or other people with trauma triggers, then I guess our whole family has been kind of doing Easter every day this week. So, I don't know, it made me stop being mad. It kind of made me happy, you know?"

Before Celia could form a reply, her phone vibrated in her pocket. Pulling it out, she saw Homer's number on the screen, "It's Dad," she whispered to Rocky and CJ. Pressing "answer" and "speaker" she grinned at her children as Homer's voice boomed across the miles, "He Is Risen!"

"He Is Risen Indeed, Daddy!" CJ and Rocky replied in unison.

A beat later, with tears in her eyes, Celia added, "Indeed."

5 ROOTS AND WINGS AT LOONSTONE LAKE
VOUME 1
CALL OF THE LOON

<u>Prologue</u>

July 11, 1974

"Shhhhhhhh, do you hear that?" Twelve-year-old Louanne Thomas stopped dead in her tracks as she waited for her cousin Christopher and best friend Molly Mears to catch up to her.

"Hear what?" Chris called out.

Breathing. Giggles. Faster breathing, almost panting. And then—crying?

Molly's eyes widened. "Someone's in there," she said, motioning to the abandoned cabin they had come to explore. "Someone's crying in there."

Chris began flicking his flashlight from side to side. Louanne grabbed his hand, forcing him to stop. "Cut it out, Chris, we don't want to be seen. I can't imagine who could be in there, I didn't see any other boat when we pulled ashore, did you?"

"No other boats on this side of the island," Chris said. "Maybe whoever it is swam over."

"That would be a long swim in the dark."

"Maybe someone lives here," Molly suggested.

"In that old abandoned cabin? Huh, I doubt it," Louanne replied. "Besides they'd still have to get on and off the island for food."

"Then maybe it's haunted. Baaahaaaahaaaa!" Chris said, holding his flashlight under his chin and making a menacing face.

"We should get out of here," Molly said.

"No way. We came here to check out that old cabin, and that's what I plan to do. This makes it even better!"

"Chris, you're being so loud. We're not s'posed to be here, remember? I don't know about you, but I don't want to be grounded for the rest of the summer," Louanne said, adding, "but I would like to check it out more. Let's go back to the edge of the water and walk around to the other side of the island—you know the side where the cabin has that broken window. Maybe we'll see something."

The three youngsters scrambled back down to the spot where they'd tied up their canoe and began creeping silently toward the other side of the island.

"Look there." This time it was Chris who stopped in his tracks, pointing to a boat moored between two rocks, "Isn't that Uncle Charlie's boat?"

Coming up alongside her cousin, Louanne took a good look at the boat. "Sure is," she said, "Can't miss that stupid mermaid he painted on the side of it. What the heck is he doing here?"

No sooner were those words out of her mouth than the cabin door opened and Uncle Charlie emerged, taking quick strides toward his boat. Someone else was with him.

"Who is that?"

"Shhhhh"

"I can't tell. But we better hope he doesn't see us." All three flattened themselves against the damp sand, hoping they could become invisible.

Uncle Charlie didn't look their way. He and his mystery partner slipped quietly into his boat and pushed off. Soon the rhythmic sounds of his paddles dipping into the water grew dimmer as the boat smoothly glided towards the Loon's Nest campground.

Chapter 1

May 7, 2014

"That hit the spot," Frank Hubert said, picking up his empty plate and walking towards the kitchen sink. "I'll wash these dishes and then I have to start grading those senior essays."

"Great. I have to run an errand before I can finish the stack of papers I'm working on tonight. Do you need anything from the market?" Louanne asked her husband as she grabbed the car keys off the hook by the door and snatched her purse from the end table.

"Just sugar for my coffee."

Forty minutes later, Louanne walked into her kitchen balancing three bags of groceries and calling out, "I'm back." She quickly put the items away and sighed as she looked at the clock. Already eight o'clock and so many papers to grade. Another late night ahead.

As she entered their shared study, Frank looked up and said, "Your cousin Christopher called while you were out. We chatted a bit about the kids' college plans and whatnot, but it sure sounded like he was calling with a mission he couldn't discuss with me. He wants you to call him back tonight if you can."

"That's odd," Louanne replied. "Chris never calls. I can't think of a time we talked by phone, except when he called to let us know Uncle Walt died last year. I sure hope no one else has died."

"I don't think so. He sounded serious but not upset or sad."

"Hmmmm, OK, well I guess I'll call him back now before I get my head into these papers. Are you making any progress on yours?"

"These are done," Frank said, pointing to a pile of papers to his left, and then indicating the pile on his right, added, "These are not. I'll get us both some tea and then I'll get back to it. Maybe you can make your call from the porch. It's pleasant out there tonight."

Louanne was just ending her call with her cousin when Frank strolled onto the porch. "That was a long call—must have been serious," he noted. "I just came to see if you needed a refill on your tea."

"Oh shoot, I didn't even drink my tea," Louanne said. "Did you finish your papers already?"

"Well, not sure if I'd call it 'already,'—it is after nine. And yes, I finished, so I'm ready to kick back and watch the rest of the ball game before hitting the sack. But I thought I'd check on you first."

"After nine? Ugh. I'm going to have to get up extra early to grade my papers. My head is spinning now and I'm too tired to read sixty-five renditions on the similarities and differences between *Romeo and Juliet* and *West Side Story*. Can you sit out here with me for a few minutes before you watch the game? I want to tell you about my call with Chris." Louanne said, shooing Inky off the porch chair next to her.

"Anything for you, dear," Frank chuckled, taking the proffered seat as the cat jumped back up and landed on his lap.

"Chris wants to sell Loon's Nest." Louanne stated. She tried to sound matter of fact, but tears sprang to her eyes suddenly as a vivid memory of sitting on the porch of Ramy and Popi's cabin at the lake flooded her mind. "I know I haven't mentioned Loon's Nest in years. Truthfully, I haven't even thought about it in years. But now, the idea of it being gone, not being in the family anymore, that's a little overwhelming."

Frank wisely gave Louanne a few quiet moments with her thoughts. The Loon's Nest Campground at Loonstone Lake in northern New England had been in her family for as long as she could remember. Her grandparents, George and Hazel Thomas, spent every summer up there, living in the family cottage and renting out the other eight cabins to families and fishermen from around the country. Their three sons, Louanne's father Henry, and his brothers, Uncle Walt and Uncle Charlie, had worked at the campground every summer of their youth, and when Henry and Walt went off to the Korean War, and Popi George died, Uncle Charlie managed it himself. Louanne, along with her siblings and cousins spent their summers barefoot and bronzed, playing in the lake, canoeing, hiking in the woods and waiting for their turn to become official Loon's Nest staffers when they turned fifteen.

Louanne smiled as she remembered feeling so small sitting in the big green Adirondack chairs on the front lawn, watching her daddy and uncles cleaning their fishing gear while the ladies played croquet. Her grandmother Hazel, called "Ramy" because her firstborn grandchild Christopher couldn't pronounce "Grammy," loved playing croquet even after she could no longer walk. Uncle Charlie faithfully pushed her around the lawn in her wheelchair so she could continue to beat anyone who challenged her to a game.

But then, in 1974, everything changed. The camp closed mid-summer, Uncle Charlie moved out west and no one talked about the camp again. The memories were packed up along with the photographs, croquet mallets and canoe paddles and locked in the attic of the family cottage at Loonstone Lake.

"What brought this on now?" Frank asked, coaxing her out of her reverie.

"College tuition," Louanne stated. "When the camp closed down in 1974, Daddy and Uncle Walt arranged for it to be put into a trust for Chris and I as the two oldest grandchildren. Chris said he never wanted to do anything with it as long as his dad was alive, but now that Uncle Walt has been gone for a year, he considers the camp to be 'the family albatross' and he says it would be good stewardship to sell it and use the funds for more important things. Like college tuition for his kids."

"The 'family albatross?' That's a pretty harsh statement. I thought you all had fond memories of your time at the camp when you were kids?" Frank probed.

"We did. I do. But no one knows what happened in 1974 and we just all understood it was never to be talked about while our parents were alive. And now that they're dead, who can we ask?"

Frank quietly reached for Louanne's hand, "Childhood memories. Potent stuff. I hope our kids have nothing but positive memories of the camping trips we took with them. Remember the time we were at Yellowstone and the bear came through our tent site?"

Louanne laughed, "I'm not sure Sidney has fond memories of that one. Luke and Robby really had him convinced the bear was going to eat him for breakfast." Now the tears streaming down her face were happy ones as memories of good times with Frank and their four children camping around the country began rolling across her mind, one after another, like gentle waves lapping the side of a canoe. "I wonder how their memories would have been different if we had camped in one place every year—you know, like the Loon's Nest—instead of taking those trips around the country?"

"I have an idea!" Frank said, "Let's tell Chris that we want to spend one last weekend at the lake before we join him in putting it on the market. We could go up for Memorial Day. We need a getaway and it would be fun. It would give you a chance to re-live some of your favorite memories and say goodbye to the camp. You know, that whole closure thing you always tell me is so important?"

"Oh what a great idea. Frank! Maybe we'll find some records of my family history up there—maybe even learn what really happened in 1974."

"Who knows what we will find? Mostly I hope we'll find some time with each other. The cots in the cabin have to be more comfortable then the air mattresses we slept on when camping with the kids." Frank added with a wink, "But for now, let's get some sleep. The ball game is over and five A.M. will roll around all too soon."

Chapter 2

May 23, 2014

"Wow! Its beautiful Lou-lou," Frank said, stepping out of the van and opening his arms expansively to take in the full picture of the campground before him.

Louanne's face did not mirror Frank's. In place of his broad smile, she grimaced. "Oh Frank, I'm not sure what I expected. I guess I was expecting it to still be the way it looked when I was a little girl." The broken windows, upended Adirondack chairs and lawn that looked like a hayfield were almost too much to take in.

"Yes, I hope Chris understands how much work it's going to take to get this place in shape to sell. But honey—the lake, the evergreens, the maples. It's spectacular. Wow, I wish you had brought me here years ago, I can just envision camping here with the kids."

Louanne barely heard him as she wandered away from the family cottage and headed towards the rental cabins. Each cabin was named for a tree. Elm. Maple. Spruce. Hemlock. Balsam. Poplar. Birch. And her favorite, Larch. Walking the rocky shore path, she noticed that some of the cabins still had canoes tethered to trees, while others were long gone. The canoe in front of Balsam had become a home for some kind of animal— raccoons maybe? And the one by Birch was cracked and broken, but hanging on.

"*Cracked and broken, but hanging on.* That should be the new theme song for the Loon's Nest Campground," Louanne mused aloud to herself as she stepped around behind Larch and into the woods, looking for the staff cabins. The path that had been there was completely overgrown, so she was picking her way through based on memories that were decades old. "Can it really have been forty years since I was last here?"

Louanne was feeling a little disoriented and lost when she heard Frank calling to her from the family cottage, "Lou-lou where did you go? We should get a few things unpacked before it gets dark." Still not finding the staff cabins, she was thankful to see Larch again.

"I must have walked in a circle," she said to herself, shaking her head. She decided to head back to where Frank was waiting for her.

As soon as Louanne stepped into the opening where the family van was parked, she saw Frank setting up the tent they'd tossed in at the last minute, "just in case" they needed it. "The floorboards are warped and dangerous in there, Lou, and there are mice droppings everywhere and some bigger droppings—maybe deer—in the kitchen. I think we'll be better off in the tent for tonight. Maybe tomorrow we can clean up at least one cabin enough to make it our base for the rest of the weekend."

"Oh, it's that bad? I should have known."

"It's OK, it's still beautiful and peaceful. We've camped in tents for years; one more night won't kill us. Can you give me a hand here, hold the stakes while I pound them in?"

An hour later, after establishing a relatively comfortable little campsite, Frank and Louanne decided to take a walk and explore the rest of Loon's Nest. The sun was beginning to set over the lake as they approached the waterfront. "Listen Frank," Louanne stood stock-still inclining her ear towards the lake. The hauntingly beautiful sounds took her breath away.

"Are we hearing the loons?" Frank, too, stood still, listening, mesmerized. "I haven't heard loons since that time we camped in northern Minnesota with Jack and Diane. Emily was just two that summer. They had just adopted their Justin and that's when we first thought about adopting, remember? Wow—so long ago! But I'll never forget that loon music."

"Come here, Frank." Louanne grabbed his hand and led him through a stand of trees towards the water. Where they stepped out from the trees, a large boulder jutted into the water. "This is my prayer rock. My grandmother, Ramy Hazel, she was the spiritual head of the family. She was the one who never let us go to bed without a Bible story, and she was up at the crack of dawn every morning reading her own worn-out Bible and praying for all of us. Ramy told me to find a place where I felt comfortable talking to God and then to visit Him there everyday. This was my place." Louanne dropped Frank's hand and climbed onto the rock. Frank stood back and snapped a picture.

"Such peace here," she continued. "I'd sit and pray and I always felt like the loons were singing their own hymns to God. Silly, I guess, but oh, how I've missed this place."

"I can see why it holds such a special place in your heart. I'm looking forward to exploring it more in the morning. Maybe one of these old canoes is still sturdy enough for us to go out onto the lake. We could paddle over to that island and back." Frank pointed across the lake to an island with a ramshackle house on it. "It looks like that house is abandoned."

Louanne followed his gaze to the island and shivered.

"What is it?"

"I'm not sure. Something about that island creeps me out. Chris and I used to paddle out there as kids, but, I don't know, something is tickling at the back of my mind. It will probably come to me."

The next morning Frank was busy brewing coffee on the camp cook stove by the time Louanne woke up. "Good morning sleepy head," he said, handing her a steaming mug, with a giant grin on his face and a twinkle in his eyes. Louanne knew he was up to something.

"What?" she asked suspiciously, raising an eyebrow and lightly blowing on the hot coffee.

"I couldn't sleep, so I walked down to your prayer rock and sat there for hours last night. I don't think I slept at all, I'm so excited."

"You sure look chipper for someone who didn't sleep. What's all the excitement about? I'm feeling a little sad myself. Being here makes me realize how much I love this place and it's making it harder to think about letting go of it."

"Let's take that canoe ride and I'll tell you my ideas," Frank said, pulling Louanne to her feet.

"Now?"

"No time like the present—Let's go!"

There was no sun on the lake; the slate color of the sky nearly matched the color of the water. As they climbed into the canoe, Louanne spotted the family of loons hugging the shoreline about a hundred yards away. "Did you know that loons are monogamous and mate for life?" she asked Frank.

"Really?"

"Yup. Learned that from Popi George. He was a hunter and fisherman and knew everything about the wildlife here at the lake. He also taught me that in loon families, the momma loons and poppa loons share equally in the responsibility of raising the young. Fascinating, isn't it?" Just then a powerful adult loon burst into the air and executed a spectacular dive below the surface of the water.

Frank paddled mid-way across the lake and then sat still. Louanne listened to the rhythmic slapping of the water against the side of the boat, waiting for Frank to share his ideas. From this vantage point, they could see the entire Loon's Nest Campground and half a dozen of the privately owned homes along the edge of the lake.

"I've been thinking about that favorite saying of yours. The one you embroidered on that wall-hanging before we adopted Robby and Sidney, 'There are only two lasting gifts we give our children – roots and wings.' – did I get it right?"

"Close enough." Louanne leaned towards Frank; the canoe rocked gently.

"We've always tried to help our kids know their roots—their birth family heritage—and roots in faith and in our family. But this place, this place represents your roots. We need to save it. It's your legacy. Let's keep it in the family! I was thinking instead of joining with Chris to sell it, we should buy out his half and keep it, rebuild it, reopen it. I have so many ideas about what we could do here—to use this place for new generations to grow deep roots and to spread their wings. Strong wings—like our friend the loon there."

"Oh Frank, I'd love to keep it in the family! But our kids are kind of past the camping stage now. Sid's in college and Robby, Luke and Em are busy with their lives, they aren't going to drop everything to come run a campground with us. And thank goodness there aren't any grandchildren just yet. So I'm not sure what you are thinking."

Frank began paddling back towards the shore. "You know how we always worry about those kids in our classes who have no family, no guidance? The kids in foster care, or the ones that have spent time in detention? They can't get summer jobs as easily as the other kids and they just seem adrift? What if we could develop a program for them? Job training. Life skills. We could hire them and save the camp at the same time."

Louanne burst into tears.

"What?" A look of bewilderment quickly replaced the exuberant smile on Frank's face.

"Oh Frank. You never knew my Popi George, but he would be so proud of you right now. He always hired what he called, 'troubled kids' to work here at the camp. If my dad said it once, he said it a million times, Popi's favorite quote was 'An honest day's work for an honest day's pay is the best way to help a kid get on the right path.' I love this idea!"

They spent the rest of the weekend sweeping, scrubbing, cleaning, dreaming and praying. By the time they got in the van to travel home on Monday afternoon, Louanne and Frank were convinced it was not only their plan, but God's own plan for them to buy out and reopen Loon's Nest.

"Just a few hurdles in our way, Frank." Louanne said as they turned off the dirt road and onto the highway, "Convincing our own kids that this is a good idea. Then convincing Chris and my siblings and other cousins." She began ticking off the challenges on her fingers.

"And don't forget coming up with the money," Frank added helpfully, "A boatload of money."

"Do you think we can pull it off? It seems impossible."

"*Impossible!*" Frank began to sing, belting out the song from the movie version of Cinderella, "*For a plain yellow pumpkin . . . *"

"*To become a golden carriage,*" Louanne joined in with a newfound lightness in her heart.

Chapter 3

May 31, 2014

"Sid's here!" Frank shouted up to Louanne as she finished dressing. She heard him dash out the front door, letting it slam in his wake. Both Louanne and Frank were eager to see their youngest son, he hadn't been home from college since Christmas break.

Louanne stepped into the kitchen just in time to be swept up into a bear hug. After the embrace, she pulled back and looked her tall, thin son up and down. "Most kids gain ten pounds in college, Sid, how did you manage to lose weight? I'm going to have to fatten you up while you're home. And this must be Liam," Louanne said, turning to the young man standing inside the doorway. "Come on in, I promise not to bite."

"Very nice to meet you, ma'am," the short, stocky young man with a flock of freckles and a shock of unruly red hair stuck his hand out awkwardly towards Louanne.

"No need to call me ma'am, although I will let your momma know that she raised you right! We're so glad you and Sid got this internship together for the summer. We're delighted to have you staying with us."

Frank and the two younger men gathered at the kitchen table where Louanne had placed a bowl of fruit and a basket of muffins. "Coffee?" Frank asked, filling four mugs. Louanne stood at the counter deveining the shrimp for her famous Shrimp and Avocado salad.

Within the hour, the other three Hubert children began arriving for the family's delayed Memorial Day barbeque.

"Need any help, Mom?" Luke asked as he fished a few grapes out of the fruit salad.

"I need your help making sure there is food for everyone else," Louanne replied, gently slapping her son's hand. "And yes, you can help. Can I get you to cut up some peppers and onions to throw on the grill? The grilled veggies go so well with the chicken. I need to put the punch together and then I think we are all set. Wonder why Emily's not here yet?"

"She texted me. She's on her way. She stopped to get ice cuz she knows you never have any," Luke said.

"Oh, I think I hear her car now. Did she say she was bringing anyone with her?"

"If you mean like Cory, the answer is no. They are not that serious mom. I think her friend Mealea is coming, though."

As if on cue, Emily and her best friend walked through the door, Em with bags of ice, and Mealea with a large Tupperware container. "I brought homemade spring rolls Mom-Lou," Mealea said, setting the container on the counter. "Half are vegan, you know, for Sid and whoever else wants vegan."

"Bless you," Louanne said, stepping around the counter to hug both girls.

~

"So, I can't believe we have a lakefront property in the family and we never knew about it. Spill the beans now, Mom. Dad." Robby said once everyone's plates were piled high with food and grace had been said.

"Yeah, spill now cuz you got a lot of 'splainin' to do," Luke added in his best Ricky Ricardo imitation.

"My grandparents owned a camp way up in a corner of northern New England called the 'Northeast Kingdom' for years and years. I spent my summers there as a child, with my siblings Karen and Brian and my cousins Chris and Janey. It was really like a piece of heaven," Louanne started. Looking at Mealea she added, "My best friend Molly used to come up there most summers, too."

"Your mom doesn't really know what happened, but the camp was closed down in the middle of the season long before any of you were a twinkle in the eye," Frank continued. "No one has used the camp since 1974, it has kind of lain fallow, but it has been held in a trust for your mom and her cousin Chris."

"Why did it close?"

"Was there a scandal?"

"All the camping we did, why didn't we go up there?"

The questions from their four adult children were flying fast and furious across the picnic table.

"After my Uncle Walt died last year, Chris started to think about selling the property. He figured the money could help him put his kids through college. So he called me to discuss it and that's when dad and I decided to go make a 'goodbye' pilgrimage to the camp last weekend." Louanne picked up the story as unexpected tears threatened to spill down her cheeks.

"I saw how much your mom loved the place and I thought we should try to keep it in the family," Frank explained, adding, "It would mean buying out Chris's share. Scraping up the money will be tough, and it would mean less for other family activities, like helping you when your car breaks down. Again." Everyone looked at Robby on that note and laughed.

"So," Louanne piped up, regaining her composure, "we wanted to hear what you kids thought before we took the plunge. Although we have already talked to Geoff Lukens at the Teacher's Credit Union about applying for a loan just to see what it would take. Chris got an appraisal done before he called me. Even though the property is in terrible shape, it is still valued at almost a million dollars, so, well, it's a lot to come up with."

"What did Geoff think?" Luke asked. Geoff's younger brother Eric was one of Luke's high school classmates. "I trust him."

"He advised us to develop a business plan. Map out how we foresee bringing the campground back to life, and what the market would be in both the near-term and down the road," Frank replied.

"Seems reasonable," Sid said. "Have you done that yet?"

"Geoff put us in touch with a young kid who specializes in business plans, his name is Deion Abernathy. We have an appointment next Tuesday," Louanne said.

"Deion's not a young kid, he's two years older than me. I went to school with his sister Diamond," Emily noted. "Deion is really smart, I might add."

"You have to hear the best part of your dad's plan," Louanne said.

"I want to create a business model that not only results in a top-of-the-line campground experience for our guests, but also provides a summer job program for youth with extra challenges in their lives. Teens who have been in foster care, or juvenile justice. Maybe teens with disabilities. I'd love you guys to help with that part of the plan and maybe serve as mentors."

"I know I'm not officially part of the family, but I think that's a brilliant plan, Poppa-Frank," Mealea said.

"You know you are part of the family, silly girl, and I do appreciate your input. What about the rest of you?" Frank looked into the faces of each of his children.

"Go for it!"

"I'd be worried about you and mom working too hard when you should be starting to enjoy life a little, but all-in-all, it sounds like a good plan."

"Can I come to the meeting with Deion?"

"When do we get to see this place?"

One by one, they each weighed in and the conversation lasted through dessert. By the time marshmallows were roasting over the coals, there was a clear consensus to go forward with the business plan and loan application.

~

Louanne curled up next to Frank in bed later that evening and said, "That went better than I thought. We didn't 'need' their permission, but it sure feels good to know they are all onboard. It makes me feel more confident that the loan will come through. I'm starting to believe this might be possible."

"We still have to convince your cousin. If he considers the camp an albatross, I wonder how he will feel about letting it stay in the family?" Frank asked.

"I've been wondering that, too. Maybe he knows more about what happened in 1974 than I do. He is two years older than me, he might have seen or heard more than I can remember. I'll call him in the morning."

Chapter 4

June 4, 2014

A mere hint of the sun was peeking out from between the two houses next door when Louanne took her morning coffee to the porch with time to spare before heading out for another day of teaching. She expected to be alone and was surprised to see Sid's friend Liam already out there, clickety-clacking away on the keyboard of his tablet.

"Good morning Liam, you're up bright and early."

"Yes ma'am, its my best time to think," He replied, looking startled.

"How are you liking the internship so far?"

"I love it. They're not just making us get coffee or sort mail. Some of my professors told us to look out for that. But they are giving us real work. It's pretty cool."

"That's wonderful, Liam. I'm so glad you and Sid became friends. He often likes to be the lone ranger, so this is new territory for him, and I thank you for sharing it."

"Yes, ma'am. I think I'll go get ready for work now. Nice talking to you." And with that, he stood to go inside the house. As he opened the door, Frank stepped out.

"Did you scare the boy off?" he asked.

"I hope not. But I was kind of hoping for a little time alone."

"OK, hint taken, I'll go back inside."

"No, stay. Let's talk for a few minutes. It's been quite a week and my head is spinning. I can't believe in the last few days we got all four of our kids, my cousins, my sister and brother to agree to the Loon's Nest plan. And that meeting with Deion yesterday—I just loved getting all of our ideas down on paper in a way that actually makes sense. It feels like God is really walking with us on this."

"I feel more like He's walking one step ahead of us and blazing the trail," Frank said. "And who knew that the hardest sell would be your brother, Brian. He doesn't even remember Loon's Nest, but he sure had lots of opinions about what should happen to it."

"Yea, that threw me too. Truthfully, I thought it would be Chris's sister Janey we'd have the most trouble with. She was always a little angry that Dad and Uncle Walt left the campground to Chris and I and not to all of the cousins equally."

"It was smart to suggest that we will pay each of your siblings and Janey a portion of the value in addition to Chris's share. Goodwill and peace for the family is always a good thing."

They sat quietly for a few moments, watching the sun splash streaks of butterscotch across the sky while three robins each staked out their hunting territories on the front lawn. A garbage truck rumbled by and two squirrels jumped from one branch to another in the neighbor's yard. Kyle Williams, the paperboy, tossed the daily onto the lawn and waved.

"What I'm most pleased about is Robby's interest in all of this,"

Frank picked up the discussion. "It was a big surprise that he wanted to come to the meeting with Deion, but he had such valuable input. I hope his enthusiasm continues."

"He really has a head for business and a heart for teens without families. He was only three when we adopted him, but it's almost like he can relate to them. In some ways, he is an old soul in a young man's body. Hard to believe he's only twenty-three."

Suddenly the door flew open as Sid and Liam dashed across the porch and down the steps to the car. Sid's hair was still wet and he was holding his tie with his teeth while he juggled car keys, tablet and briefcase with his two hands. Without so much as a nod or wave, the boys were in the car and on their way to their internship in town.

"Will that boy ever develop a sense of time?" Frank shook his head.

"Oh, he has a sense of time," Louanne answered, "It just doesn't match anyone else's."

"I suppose. Anyway, I guess that's our cue to get a move on, too. No slacking just because it's the last week of school. I'll drop our business plan and loan application off with Geoff after school while you attend that yearbook meeting and then I'll swing back over to school and pick you up."

~

June 8, 2014

"Can I help you with that?" Frank asked Imelda Collins.

"Oh thank you, dear. I don't see so well these days. Can't always tell where the curb is. Don't want to break my ankle like Lucy Bennett did last year. Poor thing." With Frank's help, the elderly woman successfully navigated the sidewalk by the church and got settled into her daughter's car.

"Thanks for helping out, Mr. Hubert," Tansey Collins called from the driver's side of the car. She had her hands full buckling two toddlers into car seats.

Stepping back, Frank noticed Geoff Lukens standing on the curb. "Good morning, Frank. Great service today, wasn't it? I thought the choir was especially good."

"Yes, that hymn has always been a favorite of mine," Frank said, adding, "But I suspect you didn't wait around just to remark on the choir."

"True. I shouldn't do this at church, I know," Geoff said, lowering his voice to a whisper. "But I wanted to give you and Louanne a heads up."

"I'm hoping you are about to say that our loan was approved, but by the look on your face, I'm guessing I would be wrong about that."

"Frank, Loon's Nest closed very abruptly in 1974 and hasn't been operated since then. It's a concern."

"We were completely open about that the first time we talked to you—what's changed?"

Geoff spoke, "I know, I know. But questions have come up about the 'Why?' of it all. Why did it close down so suddenly in 1974? Why did no one open it up again? Why didn't Louanne's family sell it years ago if no one planned to operate it? My VP wants some of these questions answered before we can proceed." Geoff clapped Frank on the shoulder and concluded, "The good news is, they are not outright denying the loan. Just tabling a decision pending some more answers."

~

June 11, 2014

Emily stood by the kitchen window at her parents' house waiting for the tall older brother of her high school friend to pull into the driveway. Just last week she'd confided to her mother about the secret crush she'd had on him throughout high school. She hadn't seen him in ten years and now he was coming to help her parents realize a dream. As soon as she saw the car, she touched up her lipstick, smoothed her hair and walked slowly to the door to greet him.

"Thank you for coming, Deion. My parents really appreciated your help last week. Now that the bank says we need more answers, we just don't know what to do. My brother Robby and I are here to see if we can help. Luke and Sid had to work," Emily spoke far too quickly as she ushered Deion into the family room.

Louanne greeted Deion and offered everyone lemonade before taking a seat next to Frank on the sofa. Robby and Deion sat in the two Queen Anne chairs and Emily perched on the ottoman looking a little like a cat waiting for a mouse to pounce upon. Two large cardboard boxes were in the middle of the floor and several old photo albums were laid across the coffee table.

"We've searched and searched through all the papers and albums we found in the attic at the family cottage at the lake," Louanne began. "We can't find a thing that helps answer any of the bank's questions. I've spoken to my cousin Chris and he swears up and down that he doesn't know anything either."

"And everyone else in the family associated with the campground in 1974 is dead," Frank said. "We're at a loss as to what to do next."

"You could hire a private investigator to get to the bottom of the story. I brought a few names of investigators our firm has worked with. These guys are reputable," Deion handed Louanne a sheet of paper with names, phone numbers and websites.

"Oh look, Frank, this one, Livingston Investigations, they are based over in Sweetland where my friends Homer and Celia Evers live. Wonder if they know these folks?"

"That will take some time, of course," Deion continued, "And I gather there is some urgency here to move things forward."

"Yes, Lou's cousin needs his share of the proceeds before school starts in September," Frank explained.

"Right, I remember that from our last discussion. So, I suggest that even if you do go ahead with the investigator, we strategize a few additional steps. We may not be able to get the exact answers the bank is seeking, but we can get them some information that should help assuage their fears."

"Really, Deion? What would that involve?" Emily spoke for the first time.

"What the bank really needs to know is if the mysterious history of the campground will impact sales today, in 2014. We can learn this two ways. First, we need to go up there to Loonstone Lake. Talk to people in the community. Perhaps conduct a focus group meeting or at least a series of interviews."

"And what is the second thing?" Robby asked.

"I know your cousin had the property appraised, but we should hire our own appraiser and inspector to thoroughly assess the property. Make sure there is nothing there that would hinder the successful execution of your business plan."

"I'm guessing you have some recommendations for that as well?" Louanne asked, holding her hand out expectantly.

~

"Look at this one, mommy is this you?" Emily held an old black and white photo in her hands. After Deion left and Robby left, Frank had stepped out to mow the lawn, but mother and daughter lingered in the living room looking through the old family photos and documents one more time.

"Oh my," Louanne laughed at the photo of a cute baby sitting in a bucket next to a large dog. "Yes, that's me, and that's Ramy and Popi's dog, Stinker. I was terrified of him—look at my face!" By now both women were rolling with laughter.

"Mom? Do you really think Deion's plan will work? I'm dying to know what really happened in 1974, but even more, I want you and dad to be able to have your dream."

"I guess it's in God's hands now," Louanne said, "But one thing is for sure, it looks like we'll get to spend some more time with Deion, and from the looks of things, that means we'll get to spend some more time with you, too!"

Chapter 5

July 11, 2014

"Pull over, right here," Louanne said to her husband as they approached the turn-off for Loon's Nest Campground. She reached into the back of the van and retrieved the bunch of yellow balloons tied to the armrest. "You go on ahead, I'll walk the rest of the way."

Louanne tied the balloons to a tree and began the three-quarter mile walk to camp. Breathing in the balsam-scented air, she pinched herself to make sure this day had really arrived. What a roller-coaster the past month had been, but with the help of Deion, Geoff, family, friends and a boatload of prayer, the day had finally come to start whipping Loon's Nest into shape before the grand opening. She relished these few quiet moments before the vehicles filled with volunteers would begin arriving.

"Cleaning supplies, check. Food to feed an army, and charcoal for the grill, check. Enough gas for the lawn-movers and other yard equipment, check." Louanne began rehearsing her checklist aloud as she walked towards camp. She was just steps away from the main entrance when a motorcycle roared past her and spun around in the dirt stopping in front of her. Stepping down and removing their helmets, the driver and his passenger burst out laughing.

"Deion and Emily, you about gave me a heart attack! You didn't say you'd be arriving on a Harley!" Louanne did her best to look annoyed, but her heart was bursting with joy to see her Emily so happy. She and Deion had become an "item" ever since the trip to Loon Lake for the community focus groups. Although that was only three weeks ago, they were already the kind of couple that finishes one another's sentences. Louanne couldn't help but dream about wedding bells in the future.

"I took the bike Mrs. H because my brother DeMonte is driving my dad's truck up here with all the paints and ladders we bought with the money donated by Sigma Pi Phi. He should be here soon," Deion said just as Frank emerged from the family cottage to join the conversation.

"What an outpouring of blessings we've received. From your fraternity, Em's employer and several churches and youth groups—we are going to be cookin' with bacon grease here soon," Frank said, clapping Deion heartily on the back.

Just then a convoy of four vehicles began pulling into the driveway led by Deion's brother DeMonte. Next came sweet little Rozene Gentry with an SUV full of girls from the Youth Acres Group home down in Sweetland. Louanne had met them recently while visiting her college roommate, Celia Evers. Rick Ellison's van filled with men from the Danville Rotary club was next and Louanne's sister Karen pulled up the rear with her family.

Louanne watched, her mouth agape, as people, coolers, cleaning supplies and cans of paint spilled out of all vehicles and the parking area began buzzing with reunions and introductions. She and Frank walked around greeting each person, thanking them for coming to the special "Loon's Nest Clean-Up Weekend" and welcoming the newcomers as they arrived. By the time Luke, Sid and Liam pulled in a few minutes later, six different groups of volunteers were ready to get to work.

Emily pulled out her camp whistle and called the crowd to order. With all of her experience during college and in her current job organizing volunteer crews for service projects, she was the perfect person to whip this group into shape. "We have four primary projects," she began, "yard work, painting, interior cleaning and minor repairs. Big repairs, plumbing and such were completed last week, so all of the big systems are in tip-top shape and you'll see we have a brand-new, up-to-code kitchen in the dining hall across the road. After the interior cleaning is finished, we have a fifth project—bed making and pillow fluffing." That drew a laugh.

"Each project has a crew leader," She continued. "I'll introduce you to the leaders and then, depending upon which project you are most interested in, you gather with the crew leader and that's where you will get further instructions and necessary supplies. Rick Ellison from Danville is in charge of the yard crew. If you want to do yard work, meet him in front of the shed over there."

"Don't let Robby get in that line!" Luke called out, ribbing his younger brother. "He's dangerous around lawnmowers—remember the time he cut his toe off?" This drew gasps and another round of laughter before Emily could continue.

"Dean Withers and DeMonte Abernathy from Sigma Pi Phi are co-leading the painting crew. There will be both inside and outside painting jobs—meet them by the white tent over there if you want to paint," Emily said and continued until all leaders had been introduced and everyone had dispersed to their chosen crew. Looking up from her checklist, she noticed an overweight teenager leaning against a tree, alone. "I'm Emily, what's your name?" she asked, walking up to him.

"Kevin," he mumbled.

"Can't find a crew that interests you?"

"I came with my youth group cuz the pastor said I should come. But I ain't no good at any of this stuff. I'm in foster care so I ain't allowed to use lawnmowers, and if I paint, I'd just make a mess."

"Forget about the mess part, is painting something you'd like to do?" Emily asked and watched the boy's eyes light up just a bit as he slowly nodded. "Super, I know there is a paint job you can do. We need the whole backside of the dining hall painted. I need someone big and strong like you to work on that. Would you be willing to give it a try? I'll make sure you have a couple helpers, you won't be alone."

"Really? You gonna trust me with a paint brush?"

"I sure will. Ready to start? Let's walk over so you can meet Dean and DeMonte and they'll get you set up."

After Emily made sure Dean welcomed Kevin, she strolled over to where her mother and Luke were setting up a refreshment tent and getting the charcoal grill started. "Mom, I have to tell you about this boy Kevin I just met. He's exactly the kind of kid dad wants to bring here to Loon's Nest. The campground isn't even open yet and dad's dream is already starting to come true. It gave me goosebumps."

"Our God is a God of goosebumps and muscle-grease," Louanne said, looking around. "Just look at all these people who showed up to help. I can hardly take it in. I do hope I planned enough food."

"Mom. Seriously. Have you ever not planned enough food? For

anything?" Luke affectionately elbowed his mom in the ribs, adding, "but they aren't going to want it raw, so let's get cooking."

~

July 13, 2014

Louanne plopped down on the couch and laid her feet across Frank's lap, a not-too-subtle hint that she was ready for a foot rub. In the distance, she could hear the loons begin their evening serenade. What an exhausting, but exhilarating, weekend it had been. Loon's Nest looked like it had received a total makeover and was now the belle of the ball. "I can't wait for Chris, Janey and Brian to see it when they come next weekend for the official 'christening!'" she said to Frank as he began kneading her aching feet.

"They won't recognize it at all. I can't remember when I have ever witnessed such a transformation. I can hardly wait to see all the roots and wings that will sprout here over the next few years."

"Me either," Louanne said, closing her eyes and leaning her head back on a small grey pillow. "My only disappointment is that those private investigators didn't get us any closer to the truth about what happened in 1974. I know the bank accepted the information we gave them, but as for me, I need to keep looking for answers. I can't abide an unsolved mystery, Frank Hubert, I just can't."

Roots & Wings at Loonstone Lake, Volume One: Call of the Loons Recipes

Louanne's Shrimp & Avocado Salad

Ingredients

2 limes, juiced, plus additional lime wedges for garnish
1 clove garlic diced
1 tablespoon olive oil

1 pound shrimp cooked, peeled, de-veined and chopped
1 medium tomato diced
1 avocado diced
1 red bell pepper diced
1 red onion diced
1 tablespoon cilantro chopped
Salt and pepper to taste
Romaine or Bibb lettuce finely chopped

Directions

1. Combine lime juice, garlic and olive oil in a bowl.
2. Add shrimp and stir to coat all shrimp pieces with lime juice mixture.
3. Add tomato, avocado, red bell pepper and red onion, stir again.
4. Add cilantro, salt and pepper, toss gently.
5. Make a bed of chopped lettuce in a pretty salad bowl
6. Top with shrimp and avocado mixture, garnish with a few wedges of lime. Serve chilled.

Pucker-up Punch

Ingredients:

10 lemons, juiced (you should have about 2 cups of juice)

1.5 cups of sugar

1 cup boiling water

7 cups cold water

1 cup unsweetened cranberry juice

2 cups seltzer water

Optional: 3 scoops of lemon, lime or raspberry sherbet

Directions:

1. Make simple syrup by mixing sugar and boiling water until sugar is completely dissolved. Set aside to cool.
2. When simple syrup has cooled, add lemon juice and stir until thoroughly mixed.
3. Pour lemon juice mixture, cold water, and cranberry juice into a punch bowl.
4. Slowly add seltzer water.
5. If desired, add 3 scoops of sherbet.

Fiesta Chicken Packets

Ingredients:

4 boneless, skinless chicken thighs or breasts
2 limes, juiced

2 tablespoons olive oil

1 15 ounce can black beans, drained
2 cups corn—can be frozen, canned or scraped off the cob
2 tomatoes, seeded and diced
2 tablespoons finely diced jalapenos or green chilies
1 clove garlic, finely diced
1 teaspoon Adobo seasoning
1 teaspoon red pepper flakes
1 teaspoon chili powder
Salt and pepper to taste

Optional: ½ cup shredded Pepper-Jack cheese and ½ cup sour cream

Directions:

1. Prepare and preheat your outdoor grill—this recipe works with a wood-based campfire, charcoal or gas grill.
2. Combine lime juice and olive oil in a bowl, add chicken thighs or breasts, toss to coat and set aside to marinate for at least 30 minutes.
3. Combine black beans, corn, tomatoes and jalapenos in a bowl.
4. Add garlic and all seasonings, stir.
5. Lay four squares of heavy-duty aluminum foil on the counter; spray each sheet of foil with cooking spray.

6. Place one chicken thigh or breast in the center of each sheet of foil.
7. Spoon a quarter of the corn and bean mixture on top of each piece of chicken.
8. Bring up sides of foil and fold to make a secure packet.
9. Place packets on grill. Grill approximately 20 minutes until chicken is no longer pink in the middle. Actual time may vary depending on the specific type of grill you use.
10. *Optional: Before serving add 1/8 cup of shredded cheese and a dollop of sour cream to each serving.*

Note: This recipe may also be made in an oven. Preheat oven to 450 degrees. Place chicken packets on a baking sheet and cook for 15-20 minutes.

-

New England Baked Beans

<u>Ingredients</u>

1 pound dry great northern or navy beans

8 cups water

2 yellow onions, cut into chunks

8 ounces salt pork, cut into cubes

½ cup Vermont Maple Syrup, Grade B

¼ cup dark molasses or dark brown sugar

3-4 cups boiling water

¼ cup ketchup

¼ cup apple cider

2 tablespoons yellow mustard

Salt and Pepper to taste

<u>Directions</u>

1. Place beans in a large pot, add water, and bring to a boil. Boil for 5 minutes and remove from heat.
2. Let beans set for 1 hour and then drain.
3. Preheat oven to 250 degrees
4. Using an old-fashioned bean pot or a Dutch oven, line the bottom with the salt pork and onion chunks
5. Add beans, maple syrup, molasses (or brown sugar) and stir

6. Pour 3-4 cups boiling water over beans and cover tightly
7. Bake for 3 hours stirring occasionally.
8. Remove from oven, uncover beans, add ketchup, apple cider, mustard, salt and pepper and stir.
9. Bake for 3 more hours, stirring occasionally.
10. When stirring if necessary you may add small amounts of additional water, a few tablespoons at a time.
11. Serve with brown bread or corn bread.

Cricket Pie

Ingredients:

1 Oreo piecrust

1 package of Oreo or similar sandwich cookies

1 pint coffee ice cream, softened

1 cup heavy cream, whipped plus additional whipped cream for garnish

Directions:

1. Break cookies into small (bite-size) chunks, reserve approximately one fourth of the cookie chunks.
2. Mix all but reserved cookie chunks into softened ice cream, stir.
3. Fold whipped cream into ice cream mixture,
4. Place ice cream mixture into piecrust.
5. Scatter reserved cookie chunks on top of pie.
6. Freeze.
7. Serve with dollops of whipped cream.